PUZZLE FOR THE
SECRET SEVEN

PUZZLE FOR THE SECRET SEVEN

Enid Blyton

KNIGHT BOOKS
Hodder and Stoughton

Puzzle for the Secret Seven

First published by Hodder and
Stoughton 1958

This edition 1992

Printed and bound in Great Britain
for Hodder and Stoughton Chil-
dren's Books, a division of Hodder
and Stoughton Ltd., Mill Road,
Dunton Green, Sevenoaks, Kent
TN13 2YA. (Editorial Office: 47
Bedford Square, London WC1B
3DP) by Cox and Wyman Ltd.,
Reading, Berks. Photoset by
Rowland Phototypesetting Ltd.,
Bury St Edmunds, Suffolk.

A catalogue record for this book is
available from the British Library

ISBN 0 340 56989 1

Contents

1 Off to the fair

'Hallo!' shouted a voice over the wall, and Scamper barked loudly at once. Peter and Janet looked up from their gardening.

'Oh, hallo, Jack!' said Peter, pleased. 'Stop barking, Scamper! Anyone would think you hadn't seen Jack for a month. Come on in, Jack. Any news?'

'Yes. Rather nice news,' said Jack, wheeling his bicycle in at the front gate. 'My mother won ten pounds at the whist drive last night – and she's given it to me to take all the Secret Seven over to the fair at Hilly-Down today. Can you and Janet come?'

'That's very decent of your mother,' said Peter, and Janet beamed. She had so badly wanted to go to the fair, but she and Peter were saving up for their father's birthday.

'There's just one thing, though,' said Jack, seriously. 'Susie will have to come too – and she's got an awful friend staying with her, called Binkie. Mother says the money's for them too.'

'Oh well – we can put up with Susie for once in a way,' said Peter. 'After all, it's not as if we were going out to solve some mystery, or are in the middle of an adventure. You tell your mother we're very, very grateful. What time shall we meet?'

'Let's go after tea, when there are crowds of people at the fair,' said Jack. 'And stay till the lights are on. I love those great flaring lights they have. Let's meet at about five o'clock at the bus-stop in the High Street. And don't pay any attention to Susie and Binkie if they giggle all the time!'

'We certainly won't,' said Peter. 'Righto, then – meet you at five o'clock. Are all the others coming?'

'Yes. I've been round to them,' said Jack, getting on his bicycle. 'We'll have at least a pound each to spend, and some of the others are bringing a bit more too. See you at five, then!'

He rode off, ringing his bell in farewell. Peter and Janet were pleased. 'We'd better ask Mother,' said Janet. 'Though I'm sure she'll say we can go – especially as we've promised to garden all day!'

Mother said of course they could go, and she would add three pounds to the money Jack's mother had given. Scamper listened to it all, wagging his tail. He looked up at Peter and gave a little whine.

'He wants to know if he can go too,' said Peter, with a laugh. 'Yes, if you can keep up with our bikes, Scamper, old thing. You're getting a bit fat, you know!'

Scamper barked joyfully. There was nothing he liked better than an outing with the Secret Seven.

'You haven't had many meetings lately, down in your shed,' said Mother. 'Has the Secret Seven broken up?'

'Oh *no*, Mother!' said Peter and Janet together, quite shocked. Mother laughed.

'Well, a week of your Easter holidays has already gone, and you haven't asked me for cakes and lemonade for one of your mysterious meetings yet,' she said. 'And I bought quite a big tin of biscuits, thinking I'd have to supply you Seven with something to nibble at your meetings!'

'Nothing's happened yet for us to call a meeting about,' said Janet. 'But we've still got two weeks' holiday left.'

'Woof!' said Scamper, agreeing heartily, and wagging his tail.

'Your life is *all* holiday, Scamper!' said Peter. 'You don't do a single stroke of work – and it's no good your trying to tell me that you helped us with the digging this morning! All *you* were doing was digging up a bone you'd hidden!'

At five o'clock quite a crowd of children arrived on bicycles at the bus-stop in the High Street. First came Peter and Janet, punctual as usual, because Peter said that as leader he must always be on time. Just after came Colin, out of breath with racing along fast in case he was late. Then came Pam and Barbara together, with George shouting behind.

'Six of us,' said Janet. 'We just want Jack and Susie and Binkie. What a name! We once had a rabbit called Binkie, do you remember, Peter? It had a dear little twitchy nose, and teeth that stuck out.'

'Here they are,' said George, as three children came cycling quickly round the corner. 'Hallo, Jack!'

'Sorry we're last,' said Jack. 'But you know what Susie is – couldn't find her purse, didn't know where her bike was . . .'

'Oooh, you fibber,' said Susie. 'You know you kept us waiting while you pumped up your front tyre. Binkie, this is the rest of the wonderful Secret Seven that I told you Jack belonged to.'

Binkie beamed all round, and Janet nudged

Peter in delight. 'She's like our rabbit!' she said, in a low voice. 'Exactly!'

Peter wanted to laugh, because Janet was right. Binkie had a funny little twitchy nose, and teeth just like a rabbit. She only needed nice long furry ears. She was a terrible chatterbox, even worse than Susie.

'Oh, hello!' she said, in a breathless voice. 'It's so nice to meet you all. Susie's told me all about you. And is this Scamper? Oh my, isn't he lovely? I've got a dog at home too, but he's a terrier, and you should see him catch a . . .'

'Shut up, Binkie,' said Jack, firmly. 'And please don't wobble on your bike when you ride with us. I never *saw* such a wobbler before!'

'Oh well, you see, it's because I always . . .' began Binkie, but nobody listened. They all rode off, chattering and laughing, Scamper running delightedly with them.

The fair was about a mile and a half away at Hilly-Down. It was in a big field, and as the children topped the last hill and looked down on the colourful sight they were full of delight.

'All those tents and stalls, and flags flying and fluttering!' said Jack, as he cycled down the hill.

'And the roundabout! I can hear its music quite

clearly,' said Janet. 'Oooh, Binkie, don't wobble so – you nearly had me off.'

They came to the entrance of the field, and went in. They stacked their bicycles carefully together in a corner, and Peter called to Scamper.

'On guard, Scamper!' he said, pointing to the nine bicycles. 'On guard, old boy!'

Scamper badly wanted to go with them, but he felt proud to be on guard. He wagged his tail and lay down by the bicycles. Peter patted him, and turned to the others.

'Now come on,' he said. 'Into the fair we go!'

2 A good time – and a shock!

The fair was very good indeed. The round-about especially was voted 'brilliant' by every-one.

'It's the *quickest* roundabout I ever knew,' said George, when they were all getting off after a very dizzy ride. 'I had to cling on to my giraffe for dear life. I was nearly swung off! Have we enough money to go again?'

'I don't want to go on again,' said Pam, trying to walk straight. 'I still feel as if I'm going round and round on my lion. Oooh, sorry, Colin – I didn't mean to bump into you. I just can't walk properly!'

Binkie was the same, and everyone laughed at the two girls, they were so dizzy. 'Let's go to the hoopla stall,' said Jack. 'But we won't let Pam or Binkie have throws, because they'll be too giddy to aim properly.'

That made both Pam and Binkie much more sensible, of course. In fact, Pam recovered so quickly that she threw best of the lot, and managed to get a hoop round a box of sweets, which she promptly shared with the others.

There was a coconut shy over in one corner, and here Peter shone, because he was an excellent thrower. He knocked down three coconuts, and the man in charge of the shy wasn't at all pleased! He handed Peter the coconuts with a very bad grace.

'However do you do it, Peter?' asked Jack, enviously. 'You *always* get a coconut when you go to a fair. And today you've got three!'

'Well, I pretend I'm bowling at a wicket,' said Peter, 'and the coconut I aim at is the row of stumps! It's easy if you think of it like that!'

Everyone immediately wanted to have another throw, but George shook his head. 'No. There's not enough money,' he said. 'Not even with Peter's extra money – unless you don't want to try anything else.'

But they all wanted to go on the big wheel, so, much to the coconut-shy man's relief, they moved off. 'Let's put these coconuts beside our bikes,' said Peter. 'I don't want to carry them about all the time. Scamper will guard them.'

Scamper was delighted to see them. He was lying by the pile of bicycles keeping an eye on everyone who passed. If anyone came a little nearer the bicycles than he thought they ought to, he stood up at once and growled. Two other dogs sat near by, admiring Scamper's fierceness. He was really feeling rather important.

Peter threw the coconuts down beside the bicycles. 'On guard, Scamper,' he said, and Scamper gave a short, sharp bark, as if to say, 'Yes, sir, certainly, sir!' He ran to the coconuts, sniffed them all over, then lay down again, keeping a sharp eye on the other two dogs.

The nine children spent every penny of their money, and then wished they had a little left to spend on some delicious-smelling hot gingerbread. This was being made in a little oven by a small, fat, gipsy-looking woman. It looked good and smelt even better.

'Want to buy some?' she asked Peter.

'Yes – but we haven't any money left,' said Peter. She laughed, and pushed a small batch of rather crumbly gingerbread squares over to them.

'Help yourselves. These are done a bit too much. I can't sell them.'

'Thanks! That's nice of you,' said Peter, and he and the others helped themselves. He saw a pram nearby, with a baby laughing in it. It was rather a dirty baby, and the pram was old, broken-down and dirty too – but the baby was such a merry little creature that no one could help watching it as they munched the delicious gingerbread.

Janet went to play with the baby, and it held out its hands, and bounced up and down in delight. 'Does the baby travel about with the fair?' Janet asked the mother.

'Oh, no. We live up in a shack on the hillside,' said the little fat woman. 'My husband goes round with the fair when it wants extra help, and when it comes anywhere in the district I sell gingerbread.' She saw some people coming up, and began to shout. 'Hot gingerbread, real old-fashioned gingerbread, straight from the oven. Twenty pence a piece, only twenty pence a piece!'

'Come on,' said Peter, looking at his watch. 'We really ought to go now. We'll just wander once more round the fair now all the lights are up.'

'I like it better when it gets dark and they light those big flares,' said Janet. 'This is just the time I love. What a pity we've got to go!'

'I think I'll stay on a bit longer with Binkie,' said Susie. 'You like the fair when it's night-time, don't you, Binkie?'

'Oh, *yes*,' gushed Binkie, her nose twitching. 'It's so – so sort of romantic. It makes me want to write poetry. Oh, do let's stay, Susie. The others can go if they want to. I might be able to write a poem about it.'

'Binkie writes marvellous poetry,' announced Susie proudly. 'She won a prize at school for it. You ought to hear her recite it.'

This was the very last thing that anyone wanted. They stared at Binkie in horror, for it was plain that she was quite prepared to recite to them then and there.

'I said it was *time to go*,' said Peter, in a very determined voice. 'And you and Binkie are to come too, Susie. We can't leave you here alone.'

'Oh yes you can. *I* don't belong to your silly Secret Seven,' said Susie at once. '*I'm* not under your orders.'

'Well, you're under *mine*,' said Jack firmly. 'And you know that Mother said you were to come back with *me*. And we are going RIGHT NOW!'

Susie said no more, but she scowled. 'She'll pay us back for this,' said Jack to Peter. 'Good thing we haven't a meeting coming on – she and Binkie would try to spoil it! Come *on*, Susie!'

They collected their bicycles from a delighted Scamper, and set off back home again. But on the way up the hill that led from the fair, George spied something that astonished him – a great light on the hillside, not far to the left.

'What's that?' he shouted, and stopped for the others to catch him up. 'Look – flames – and smoke! It's a house on fire!'

'Goodness, yes – we'd better see if we can help!' said Peter. 'Look, there's a telephone box just there, on the other side of the road, George. I'll telephone the fire brigade, while you others cut across the field-path there, and see what's happening. Hurry up!'

He rode to the telephone box and went inside, while the others opened the field gate and then rode at top speed up the narrow path that led to the fire. *Was* it a house burning fiercely – it didn't look as if much could be saved!

In the telephone box Peter asked for the fire brigade, and spoke urgently into the telephone mouthpiece. 'Hallo! Fire brigade? There's a fire up here on Hilly=Down Hill. It looks pretty fierce. Right – we'll stay here till you come!'

3   The fire at Hilly-Down

Peter let the telephone-box door swing shut, jumped on his bicycle, and cycled along the same path as the others. He caught them up as he came to the fire, and stared in horror. Whatever had stood there on the hillside was almost burnt out!

'What was it? A house?' he asked, shielding his eyes from the fierceness of the roaring flames. 'I hope no one was in it!'

'A ginger cat was the only live thing we saw,' said George, looking very solemn. 'It shot by us as we came up. It must have been a small house, Peter. Did you get on to the fire brigade?'

'Yes. They're coming. But it will be too late,' said Peter. 'Janet, don't cry. I don't expect there was anyone in the place.'

'Well – it must have been old and rotten to go up as quickly as that,' said Colin. 'What a crackling and roaring! Look out, Barbara – there are bits of burning stuff blowing about still.'

Peter took Jack with him, and the two boys anxiously walked all round the burning house, trying to see if there was anything they could do. But there was nothing to be seen but flames, now dying down a little, and tumbled, smoking pieces of wood. No wonder the poor old cat had been terrified!

Then came the sound of a loud siren, and Colin called out in excitement. 'The fire-engine! Hasn't it been quick? Well, they can't help seeing at once where the fire is!'

'We left the field gate open, didn't we?' said George, and Peter nodded. 'Yes – and look, the fire-engine's coming through it now. Gosh, I wish *I* could drive it!'

The fire-engine came slowly up the narrow, rutted path, gleaming brightly in the light from the roaring fire. 'Anyone know if there's a well?' shouted a fireman, leaping down to unroll a long hose-pipe.

'There's a stream running down the hill just here!' called Jack, and the firemen went over to it. In less than a minute they were playing water on the flames, and a great sizzling noise arose.

'Like a million bacon rashers frying at once,' said Janet in wonder, and she was right!

'Did you see anyone about?' asked one of the firemen, as the flames died down under the water.

'No. Nobody,' said Peter. 'But the whole place

was on fire when we came up – nobody could have been saved if anyone *had* been in there. But surely they would have run out, wouldn't they?'

'Might have been children asleep there,' said the man shortly. 'Whose is this shack?'

Nobody knew – but just then Peter saw someone hurrying up the field-path, wheeling something in front of her that bumped wildly over the ruts.

'It's the woman who was making gingerbread at the fair!' cried Janet. 'Oh – she said she lived in a shack on the hill-top. It must be *her* place! Poor, poor thing!'

It *was* the gingerbread woman. She came up quite breathless, her eyes staring in fright, the baby being almost bumped out of its pram.

'My Benny!' she shouted. 'Where is he? I left him here.'

'Well, Mam – we haven't *seen* anyone about,' said the chief fireman, and a little shiver of horror went through the children. No! No, surely no one could have been in that burning shack!

'Benny, Benny, Benny! Where are you, my little Benny?' screamed the woman. And then, to everyone's enormous relief, a child's high voice answered shakily from somewhere.

'Mammy! Mammy! Mammy!'

'He's safe,' said the little gingerbread woman, and tears ran down her cheeks. 'I'll go find him. He won't come out while everyone's staring round. He's in the bushes somewhere, my little Benny.'

She took the baby out of its pram, and carrying him in her arms, she hurried in the direction of a row of thick bushes a little way below the still-burning shack. 'Benny!' she called. 'Benny! Mammy's here. Everything's all right, love.'

And then, quite suddenly, it seemed as if there was a whole crowd of people staring at the dying fire – people who had left the fair, seen the flames, and come hurrying in at the open gate. Perhaps the woman's husband was there too? The children hoped so. Then he could comfort the poor little woman.

'What will they do for the night?' wondered Janet. 'Where will they sleep?'

'Oh, someone will lend them a barn, or take them in for the night,' said one of the firemen, busy rolling up the hose. 'It's a mercy no one was hurt. You kids go along home now. Thanks for letting us know.'

'I wish we'd some money left,' said Jack,

thinking that the money his mother had given him would have been a godsend to the ginger-bread woman just now.

Two policemen arrived, and one began taking notes. The other moved the crowd away. 'Move along, please,' he said. 'The fire's over. We can't do anything more. Will you move along, sir, please? And you too, madam?'

He came to the little crowd of children, still standing there with Scamper, feeling rather miserable.

'Are you the kids who warned the fire brigade?' he said. 'Well, that was good work on your part. But get along home now, please. You can't do anything more.'

'What will happen to the poor woman and her children now?' asked Peter. 'I mean – she must have lost everything in the fire.'

'We'll look after her and the family,' said the policeman, stolidly. 'She'll be all right. That was only an old shack they lived in, not a house – they didn't have much of anything. You go home now, please, and let us do what we can for the woman.'

The fire-engine departed with its siren blaring, trying to make the crowd get out of its way. The children found their bicycles and wheeled them to the gate, Scamper following, wondering if they were going home. What an evening!

They all mounted their bicycles and rode along the road, very silent. Even Susie found nothing to say. Binkie began to talk first, the words suddenly pouring out.

'I've never seen a fire before, I've never seen a fire-engine so close. Ooh, wasn't it exciting? I've never . . .'

'Be quiet,' said Peter. 'You make it sound as if it was a sort of treat! Think of that poor woman!'

'Yes. *I'm* thinking about her too,' said George. 'I say, Peter – I think we ought to call a meeting of the Secret Seven, and see if we can't plan something to help her. What about tomorrow morning at ten o'clock?'

'Fine idea!' said Peter, really pleased. 'I was just thinking the same thing myself. Secret Seven, those are your orders – be down in our shed, ten o'clock tomorrow morning.'

'Susie and me too?' said Binkie, thrilled.

'No,' said Peter. 'ONLY the Secret Seven. Susie – do you hear that? ONLY the Secret Seven!'

4 Secret Seven meeting

Next morning, sharp at five to ten, Peter and Janet were down in their shed. On the door were the letters S.S., and everything was ready inside – boxes to sit on, some biscuits on a plate, and lemonade to drink.

'I hope everyone remembers the password, and their badges,' said Peter. 'It's rather a long time since we had the last meeting.'

'Wuff!' said Scamper, suddenly wagging his tail. Janet gave a squeal of laughter.

'*Scamper* knows it! He said it! Yes, Scamper, you've remembered the password – it was Wuff! Clever dog!'

Footsteps came up the path to the shed, and Scamper gave a little whine of welcome. He knew it was George. A knock came on the door, and a low voice said, 'Wuff!'

'Enter!' called Peter, and George came in, grinning, wearing his badge on his coat.

'I nearly forgot the password,' he said. 'But luckily I'd written it down in my diary! Here comes someone else.'

It was Pam and Barbara. They knocked, and Peter called out immediately, 'Password, please.'

'Peter, we're not quite sure if it's Wuff or Woof,' said Pam's anxious voice.

'Wuff!' said Scamper at once.

'You're *not* to give the password away, Scamper,' said Janet, shocked. Barbara and Pam giggled outside the door. 'Thanks, Scamper. Wuff, Peter!'

'Come in,' said Peter. 'Just by the skin of your teeth, though! Who's that coming now?'

'Jack and Colin,' said Pam, as the door shut on her and Barbara. 'Oh, it's good to be here again, in our shed!'

Knock-knock!

'Password!' called Peter. 'And DON'T yell it.'

'We've forgotten it,' said Colin, in a very apologetic voice. 'I mean – it's so long since we had a meeting, and . . .'

'Can't let you in!' said Peter sternly.

'Oh, don't be such an idiot, Peter,' said Jack angrily. 'You know I daren't write our password down in case Susie finds it – and it's awfully difficult to remember it when we have had so many. I know it's something to do with a dog. Is it Whiskers?'

'Wuff, wuff, wuff,' said Scamper, and Pam

gave a squeal of delight. Then a voice came from somewhere in the bushes outside.

'The password is Wuff, Jack, Wuff!' and then came a burst of very loud laughter from two people.

'SUSIE! BINKIE! I TOLD you not to follow me!' cried Jack angrily. 'How do *you* know the password?'

'Oh, come in, come in,' said Peter, opening the door. Jack and Colin went in, looking angry, and Peter went over to the bushes. He spoke sternly to the two giggling girls behind them.

'Spoil-sports! Go and giggle somewhere else. If you are here in two minutes' time I shall take the hose-pipe and water this bush thoroughly. And I *mean* that!'

There was a scuffling noise, and the two girls ran off, still giggling. Susie knew that Peter meant what he said, and she didn't want to be hosed! Peter went into the shed and slammed the door.

To everyone's great relief, he said nothing at all about passwords. 'Now,' he said, taking his place on his box. 'About this business of the fire. I've . . .'

But before he could go on, Scamper began to bark madly. He ran to the door and scraped at it, still barking.

'Scamper! What's all this row about?' demanded Peter. 'If it's those two girls again you're to go and chase them away. Do you hear?'

Scamper was delighted to see Peter opening the door. He dashed out at once, and the Secret Seven looked after him to see if he was chasing Susie and Binkie.

But he wasn't. He was dancing round two legs in corduroy trousers, his tail wagging in delight.

'Oh, it's Dad's shepherd,' said Peter, in surprise, and called to the fine-looking old man on the nearby path. 'Hallo, Matt! Did you want my father? He's gone to market, I'm afraid.'

'Oh. I was afraid he'd be gone,' said old Matt, taking his cap off and scratching his thatch of grey hair. 'Well – maybe you'd give him a message for me, Peter?'

'Yes, of course,' said Peter. 'What is it?'

'Well, you probably know there was a fire last night over on Hilly-Down,' said Matt, 'and Luke Bolan and his wife had their shack burnt out, and they've nowhere to go . . .'

'Yes – we all saw it,' said Peter soberly. 'And I telephoned for the fire brigade, Matt.'

'You did? That was smart of you, Peter,' said Matt. 'Well, now, I've got an idea to put to your father – but you say he's at the market?'

'Yes. He won't be home till after dinner,' said Peter. 'What's your idea, Matt?'

'There's an old caravan up by my sheep-hut,' said Matt. 'I lived in it before your father built me my hut, and I only use it now to store my goods in. Proper broken-down old thing it is – but it would house Luke Bolan and his wife and kids for a bit, Peter, if your father would let him use it. They haven't anywhere to go, you see?'

'Oh, I'm *sure* my father would let them have it,' said Peter, and Janet nodded at once. 'Anyway, let's go and ask Mother. She'll know if Dad would give permission.'

So the whole of the Secret Seven, with old Matt and Scamper too, went up the garden-path and round the house to where Peter's mother was weeding her lettuce bed. She was most surprised to see them with the shepherd.

'Why, Matt!' she said. 'Is anything the matter?'

Matt told her what he had said to Peter, and she listened carefully. 'Of course the Bolans can have the caravan until they can find somewhere else,' she said. 'I know my husband would say that. That poor woman – all her things burnt up like that. We'll certainly have to do something to help her. You go back to the Bolans, Matt, and tell them they can move into the old caravan at once.

You can take your things out and store them in your own hut for a time, can't you?'

'Oh yes,' said Matt. 'And I can give them a rug, and lend them my little old table.'

'We'll see what we can do too,' said Peter's mother, and she turned to the Secret Seven. 'Will you let me come to your meeting for once?' she said. 'Because I think we can all help in this – and if I'm there I can help you to make sensible plans. It's a thing we must do together.'

'Of course, Mother!' said Peter, delighted. 'Come along now, this very minute! We'd LOVE to have you!'

5   All kinds of plans!

The Secret Seven filed into the shed after Peter and Janet's mother. Peter shut the door.

'I'm glad you didn't ask me for the password, Peter,' said his mother, smiling. 'Dear me, I do feel important, coming to one of your meetings. It's very nice of you to let me.'

'We're very pleased, Mother,' said Janet, and all the others nodded in agreement. Everyone liked Peter and Janet's kind, generous mother.

They began to talk about the fire, and the homeless Bolans.

'There's Luke Bolan, Mother, who goes round with the fair,' said Peter, 'and there's Mrs Bolan, who visits any fair that comes into the district, and makes hot gingerbread to sell. We hadn't any money left to buy it, but she gave us all some!'

'That was really very kind of her,' said his mother surprised.

'And there's a dear, smiley little baby,' said Pam. 'Rather dirty, but a darling.'

'And there's a boy called Benny,' said Janet.

'We haven't actually seen him, Mother. He was in the shack last night when it was burnt down, but he ran out and hid in the bushes. Poor Mrs Bolan was so afraid he would be inside the burning shack.'

'Yes. You told me last night,' said her mother. 'Well, now, let's think. I suggest that each of you should go home and tell your mothers about what has happened – and tell them that we are going to lend the old caravan to the Bolans, but that as all their things were burnt, we want to try and give them as many really necessary things as we can . . .'

'Do you mean kettles and things?' asked Pam.

'Yes – and perhaps an old mattress to sleep on,' said Peter's mother. 'There won't be room for a bed, of course. A folding chair would be a good idea – and a small mattress perhaps for the little boy and the baby. They will want food too.'

'Well, I'm really glad that the Secret Seven have something to do,' said Peter, pleased. 'It makes us much more of a real club then. What can *you* give, Mother?'

'There's an old mattress in the loft,' said his mother, thinking hard. 'And I can send up at least one saucepan – and I've an old blanket, and . . .'

'Well, if all our mothers can find something or

other we'll be able to make that caravan really cosy,' said Janet, looking forward to the job. 'I vote that everyone goes home after this meeting, and finds out what he or she can bring – and then comes back here to another meeting as soon after dinner as possible . . .'

'And we'll draw up a list of things, and choose what we think Mrs Bolan will need!' said Peter. 'Mother can help in that, can't you, Mother?'

'Oh yes!' said his mother, smiling. 'And when we've decided what to take we'll get the farm-van, and pile everything into it. We'd better take a scrubbing-brush or two, because I expect that old caravan will need cleaning.'

'This *is* going to be fun,' said Barbara. 'I'm good at cleaning! I only hope Mrs Bolan won't be there, because it would be wonderful to see her face when she comes to the van, and sees it all clean and furnished ready for her!'

'Oooh yes – I'd like to get it all quite perfect,' said Pam. 'Shall we go off home now?'

'Yes,' said Peter. 'The sooner the better! Now mind you tell your mothers what *my* mother has said – and I bet they'll all rush round and see what they can find.'

The Seven stood up, excited, and Scamper wagged his tail eagerly, jumping up at Peter. 'Do you want to help too, old fellow?' said Peter. 'Well, we'll take you with us! Now remember, Secret Seven – back here after dinner – say as near half-past two as possible. And REMEMBER THE PASSWORD!'

'Wuff!' said the rest of the Seven at once, and made Scamper bark in delight.

'Thank you, Mother, for coming to our meeting,' said Janet, hugging her mother. 'We'll bring you our lists this afternoon and let you say which things would be best to take up to the old caravan. Won't Matt be surprised to see us?'

'He certainly will,' said her mother. 'He's a kind old fellow!'

Everyone cycled home, eager to tell their mothers about the morning's meeting. Peter and Janet went to find the mattress in the loft. Yes, there it was, rolled up in thick brown paper, and tied with string. They dragged it to the trap-door of the loft, and let it slide down the ladder – BUMP! It landed at the bottom very suddenly and Scamper tore down the stairs in a great fright.

Mother went to her linen cupboard, and her blanket store, and found two old sheets and a blanket, warm and cosy. She chose a saucepan from the kitchen, and a teapot and jug from the dresser there. She rummaged out an old oil-stove too, to air the caravan.

Peter and Janet carried everything to the hall, and stored it there ready for when the farm-van called that afternoon, as Mother had arranged.

Just before half-past two the other Secret Seven members arrived, each with a list or some notes scribbled in a notebook.

Nobody forgot the password this time, and Scamper was really very funny when they all arrived at the shed. He said 'Wuff' before they did!

Peter collected the lists, and read them over. 'Gosh – your mothers have been really generous!' he said, pleased. 'Everyone's offered a blanket – and our mother did too. Let's take the lists to her, and let her decide which things will be best for the caravan. At this rate we'd have enough to furnish a dozen caravans!'

They took the lists to Peter's mother, and she checked them quickly with a pencil, crossing off duplicated articles.

'This is fine!' she said. 'Did you arrange to have the things ready, all of you?'

'Oh yes,' said everyone.

'Very well – I think I can hear the farm-van outside now,' said Peter's mother. 'We'll pack our own things into it – and then collect what we want from the other houses. Come along!'

It was fun going round in the van and collecting so many things. Everyone's mother was very kind, and said that they were pleased to think that the Secret Seven was doing such a fine job.

'And now we'll drive up to the old caravan,' said Peter's mother. 'And really set to work! We're going to have some fun!'

6 An afternoon of hard work!

'Did Susie and Binkie try to interfere, Jack, when you asked your mother for a list of things she could spare?' said Janet.

'Oh yes – and they were very cross when I said it was Secret Seven business,' said Jack. 'I told Susie there was nothing to stop her saving up a bit of money and buying something on her own. But she always wants to butt in on the Secret Seven!'

'I think perhaps you might have let them, just for once,' said Peter's mother.

'But, Mother – you don't understand,' said Peter at once. 'If we let Susie in just ONCE we'd never get rid of her. And, anyhow, we don't want eight people. We're the Secret *Seven*.'

The farm-van stopped at a field-gate, and Peter jumped down to open it. A grassy road led round the hill to where old Matt the shepherd had his hut and kept his sheep.

The van jolted slowly over the rough road, and the kettle and saucepans rattled and clanked inside. Everyone was sitting on the two old

mattresses and blankets – it was quite comfortable! At last the van jolted to a stop, and the driver
called out, 'We're as near the caravan as I can get.
And here comes old Matt.'

The shepherd opened the door of the van and
smiled all over his face as he looked inside and saw
so many people.

'Why, you've all come,' he said. 'That's very
kind of you! And what a lot of goods! That old
caravan won't know itself. I've been cleaning it up
a bit, but it's still pretty dirty.'

'We'll soon make it nice and clean!' said Janet,
jumping out. 'Come on, Mother!'

How hard they all worked that afternoon! They
washed and scrubbed and swept. Peter mended
two shelves to hold pots and pans. George stacked
the mattresses neatly rolled up, inside the caravan.
'It will be quite easy for Mrs Bolan to untie them
tonight!' he said.

Matt came back again about two hours after.
He had been rounding up some of the sheep, and
his old dog was with him. Scamper ran to him to
play, but the sheepdog lay down, put his nose
down between his paws, and shut his eyes.

'He can't be bothered with you, Scamper!' said
Peter, grinning at the surprised spaniel. 'No –
leave him alone. He's run for miles, getting the

sheep in, and he's tired. Matt – have you been able to tell the Bolans about this caravan yet?'

'Yes, I have,' said Matt. 'They were that pleased. Mrs Bolan wouldn't believe it at first. I didn't tell her you were going to furnish it, though. I thought that would be a nice surprise. She'll be along any time now.'

'Well – we've just about finished,' said Peter. 'Come and look, Matt.'

Matt could hardly believe his eyes when he saw the spick-and-span caravan, looking so cosy inside. He stared in wonder.

'There now – who'd have thought it?' he said. 'And your father talked of chopping it up for firewood next winter!'

'There's Mrs Bolan, look – with the old pram!' said Janet. 'And the little boy. She's got something piled on the pram – two loaves of bread and a few parcels. Oh, poor things, of course, all their food was burnt too! We never thought of bringing any for them!'

'Yes, we did,' said George. 'My mother sent a few tins. I've put them on the shelves that Peter mended. I expect Mrs Bolan will be sure to have brought milk for the baby.'

'We could get the shepherd to bring up milk each morning,' said Peter. 'Couldn't we, Mother?'

Mrs Bolan wheeled the pram towards them, looking surprised and a little scared to see so many people outside the old caravan. She smiled nervously. Matt went up to her in his slow, kindly way, speaking to her as if she were one of his nice old sheep.

'Come along now, Mrs Bolan, don't you be afraid, we're all friends here. This is the caravan you can have, and they've worked hard to make it really cosy. Take a look inside.'

Peter's mother came forward. 'We were so sorry to hear of the fire last night,' she said. 'Oh, what a dear little baby! And what's the little boy's name?'

But as soon as Benny felt her hand on his head he turned and fled away, hands outstretched in front of him, stumbling as he went. Janet started after him.

'Leave him be,' called Mrs Bolan. 'He's so scared now, poor lamb, what with the fire and all!'

Janet stopped. The boy, about eight years old, was small for his age, and looked a little strange. He had enormous dark eyes that stared rather blankly at them, and a shock of very black, curly hair round his small brown face. He made his way into a bush and crouched there, peering out like a small animal, listening to everything that was said.

Mrs Bolan was now admiring the caravan. 'Why, there's everything we want!' she said, looking round in pleasure. 'Even tins on the shelf! And clean as a new pin too! It's really kind of you to do all this for me. I cried my eyes out last night when that old shack of ours went up – a nasty place it was, cold and draughty, but it was our home.'

'When's your husband coming?' asked Peter, hoping to see Luke's pleasure too.

'Oh Luke – Luke's real upset,' said Mrs Bolan, looking worried. 'We lost a few precious things in that fire, you see. I lost my sewing-machine, and Luke lost his banjo and . . .'

'Oh – does he play the banjo?' said Colin. 'So does my uncle. What a pity it was burnt.'

The baby began to cry, and Mrs Bolan bent over her. 'I must give her some milk,' she said, 'and then I'll settle into the van. My, we're lucky. I'll send Luke down to thank you properly as soon as I can.'

'Shall we go now?' said Peter, and his mother nodded. She turned to Matt.

'You can bring up some milk for the baby each day, can't you, Matt?' she said to the kindly old shepherd, and he nodded.

'Well, good-bye then, Mrs Bolan,' said Peter, and everyone called out some little message too. 'Good luck! We hope the caravan will be comfortable! Tell us if there's anything else we can do!'

Peter went over to where Benny was hiding, 'Good-bye, Benny,' he said, but the strange little boy didn't answer. His great dark eyes wandered up to Peter's face, and yet Peter felt as if he was not really looking at him. What a curious child!

7 *Susie and Binkie are a nuisance*

As the Secret Seven went down the hill in the farm-van, glad to have done a really good job, they saw a man in the distance, walking slowly up. 'I bet that's Luke Bolan,' said Janet. 'I hope he'll be pleased when he sees what we've done for him.'

'I expect he will,' said her mother. 'But you must remember that even though he has a roof over his head now, he and Mrs Bolan have lost every one of their possessions – except that old pram! And it's a terrible thing to lose things you have had for years and years – like Luke's banjo.'

'Are they expensive?' asked Jack.

'Good gracious yes!' said Colin. 'My uncle paid a mint of money for his!' And he began to pretend that he was playing a banjo, strumming with his fingers and making a banjo-like noise that made everyone laugh.

'Do we have another meeting soon?' asked Barbara. 'I wish we could. It was nice to have the two we've just had.'

'Well, let's,' said Peter. 'Even though there isn't anything to have a meeting about, we could talk and have a bit of fun. Mother, can we get out of the van now and walk over the fields? It's such a nice afternoon.'

'Yes – and if you'd all like to come back afterwards to a late tea, I'll have it ready for you,' said his mother. 'You really have worked very hard, and you must be getting hungry already! I'll telephone to tell the other mothers.'

'Oh Mother! You really are a pet!' said Janet, and everyone agreed. 'Of course we'd like tea – what shall we have? Eggs? Ham?'

'Wait and see,' said her mother, laughing. 'Well, out you all get, and I'll drive on alone. Good-bye for an hour or two!'

The Seven leapt out of the van, Scamper too, and set off across the fields. It was a wonderful spring day, with the birds singing madly and primroses everywhere. Cowslips nodded on the hillsides too, and celandines shone out from the ditches.

'They're so shining-bright that they look as if they've been polished,' said Barbara.

A voice suddenly hailed them, and the Seven stopped. 'Ahoy there! Wait for us!'

'Bother! It's Susie and Binkie,' said Jack in

disgust. Sure enough it was – and they came leaping down the hill at top speed.

'Hallo! What happened about the caravan?' yelled Susie.

They told her, and she and Binkie listened with interest. 'You might have let us help!' said Susie reproachfully. 'Even though we don't belong to the Secret Seven.'

'Well, we said you could buy the Bolans anything you wanted to,' said Janet. 'Why don't you? You could take it up to the caravan yourselves.'

'Well, we jolly well will,' said Susie. 'Can we come with you now, or are you the high-and-mighty Secret Seven again, all on your own?'

'Don't be an idiot,' said Peter. 'You can see we're not holding a meeting just at this moment, so of course you can come with us.'

'Binkie's made up a poem,' said Susie, with a sudden little giggle. 'All about the Secret Seven.'

'Well, we don't want to hear it,' said George, feeling quite certain that it wouldn't be a very polite one.

'It's got a chorus,' said Susie. 'Hasn't it, Binkie? Let Binkie say the poem, Peter, and we can all join in the chorus.'

'Don't you let her, Peter,' said Jack, at once.

'You've no idea how rude Susie and Binkie can get when they put their heads together.'

But Susie was not going to be stopped, nor Binkie either. Binkie began to chant lines in a loud, sing-song manner, dancing about in front of them.

> 'Oh see the Secret Seven
> So very smug and pi,
> Eyes turned up to Heaven,
> When they come walking by!
> They think they're very clever,
> Alas, we don't agree,
> We think the Secret Seven
> Are silly as can be!

'*Chorus, please* . . .' And here Susie joined in at the top of her voice –

> 'Silly as can be, Silly as –'

But that was too much for the Secret Seven. With one accord they ran at the irritating Binkie and the aggravating Susie, yelling loudly.

'How dare you make up that song! Shut up! You horrible girl! Be quiet! We'll . . .'

But Susie and Binkie were racing away at top

speed, laughing at the anger of the Secret Seven. 'Serves you right for not letting us help this afternoon!' yelled Susie, stopping for a moment. 'You just look out for us! We'll pay you back for that!'

Then off they raced again. 'I thought this would happen,' said Jack gloomily. 'I'm very sorry about it – but I can't help having Susie for my sister. As for Binkie – think what you'd all feel like if you had to have a girl like her staying a whole week with you!'

'It's a very rude and untruthful song,' said Barbara, who always hated being made fun of.

'It's just a *little* bit funny too,' said George, but nobody would agree with him. They were now walking beside a field where a scarecrow stood, and stopped to have a look at him. A rook stood on his old black hat, and he looked very comical.

The wind waved his torn old tweed coat about and made him seem alive. 'He's got Daddy's old trousers on,' said Janet, with a laugh. 'The ones Mummy didn't like because they were too light and showed the dirt so much. And someone's tied a dirty scarf round his neck. It looks like the one our cowman used to wear – red with white spots!'

The rook bent over the scarecrow's face and pecked it. 'Shoo!' shouted Peter indignantly.

'You're supposed to be scared of him. Shoo, rook shoo!'

The rook gave two loud caws that sounded exactly as if it was laughing, spread its big black wings, and flew off slowly, cawing as it went.

'I bet it's saying something rude – like Binkie,' said George. 'I say, I'm awfully hungry now. What about that tea your mother promised us, Peter?'

That made them all hurry off at once. Eggs, ham, cold sausages, cheese, a fruit cake – they could eat the whole lot. So could Scamper. WUFF–WUFF!

8   Matt has surprising news

The tea was ready by the time the Seven poured into the farm-house. They washed and made themselves tidy and then settled down happily at the table. What a spread!

'Cream cheese!' said Jack, in delight.

'Ham and eggs!' said Pam hungrily. 'My favourite!'

'Now just help yourselves,' said Peter's mother, smiling round. 'You deserve a treat after all your good work this afternoon. I saw your sister Susie and that friend of hers as I came home, Jack, and nearly asked them in too.'

'Mother! What an *awful* idea!' said Peter, helping himself to two cold sausages, a hard-boiled egg, and a slice of ham. 'That girl Binkie made up a very rude song about us. If you'd asked her in she might quite well have had the nerve to sing it at the tea-table.'

'I'd throw the cream cheese at her if she did,' said Jack, quite fiercely.

'Oh no you wouldn't,' said Peter's mother at

once. 'I don't make cream cheese for that kind of thing. Colin, you haven't taken nearly enough ham.'

'He's dreaming!' said Pam, giving him a nudge. 'Wake up, Colin – whatever are you thinking of?'

'Well, actually, I suddenly thought of a sort of poem about Binkie,' said Colin, blinking his eyes suddenly, as if he were coming out of a dream.

'A poem! Surely *you* don't write poems, Colin!' said Janet, amazed. 'How does it begin?'

'Well, it begins like this,' said Colin, and then changed his mind. 'No, I'd better not tell you.'

That made everyone press him all the more, of course, and at last he grinned and recited a few lines, a little afraid that Peter's mother, who was listening, might not approve.

'Oh Binkie has the habit.
 Of a funny little rabbit,
 Twitching up and down her little nose . . .'

The next line was lost in gales of laughter. 'Oh Colin – that's *exactly* Binkie!' cried Jack in delight. 'I shall recite it to her whenever she and Susie start that awful Secret Seven song.'

'How does it go on, Colin?' asked Janet, looking at him in admiration.

'Well, I've only got as far as two more lines,' said Colin.

> 'And in her mouth beneath
> Are little rabbit teeth . . .

I can't think of the last line yet!'

'It doesn't sound awfully kind,' said Peter's mother, and that made Colin go red and say no more.

'Well, but Susie and Binkie aren't kind either,' argued Janet. 'Let's think of a last line:

> 'And in her mouth beneath,
> Are little rabbit teeth . . .'

'No, don't,' said Colin, anxious not to displease Janet's mother. He frowned hard at Janet, and tried to kick her under the table, but only succeeded in kicking poor Scamper, who gave a loud and indignant yelp.

'Oh sorry, Scamper, sorry!' said Colin, and slid under the table to comfort Scamper – and to change the subject too!

'Well, that was a simply delicious tea, Mother,'

said Peter when the meal at last came to an end. 'I wish I could begin all over again, but I can't.'

'It's funny – but when I tasted that cream cheese at the beginning of the meal I thought it was just about the nicest thing in the world,' said Pam. 'But now I can't even bear to look at it!'

'We'll help wash up,' said Barbara.

'Oh thanks,' said Janet. 'Shall we *all* wash up, Mother? We'll be very, very careful.'

'Yes. That would be nice of you,' said her mother, and took up her mending while the Seven went in and out, taking the dirty dishes to the kitchen.

'We'll have a meeting tomorrow, if everyone approves,' said Peter, wiping the dishes carefully. 'Can you all come at ten?'

'No. I've got to go on errands,' said Pam. 'I could come at eleven though.'

It turned out that eleven o'clock was all right for everyone, so it was duly arranged. 'We'll have to have a different password,' said Peter, 'because Susie and Binkie know the last one.'

'Wuff,' said Scamper, looking up.

'Yes, that's right. You really are too clever for words, Scamper!' said Peter, grinning. 'Well – you can choose the next one. Go on – tell us what you'd like.'

'Thump, thump, thump,' went Scamper's tail on the floor, as he looked up happily at Peter. He did so love being talked to.

'Thank you, Scamper. "Thump" is our next password,' said Peter gravely, and everyone laughed. 'I don't somehow think anyone will forget that!'

Nobody did, of course, and next morning when the knocks came on the closed shed door, where Peter and Janet awaited the others, the password was said at once. 'Thump!'

And each time it was said Scamper thumped his tail joyfully on the floor of the shed. He had never chosen the password himself before, and he felt very, very proud!

Soon all the Seven were sitting down in the shed, talking. They wondered how the Bolans were getting on in their caravan. They wondered if Matt had remembered to take up a bottle of milk when he called for his own that morning. Then George asked Jack if Susie and Binkie knew he had come to the meeting.

'No. I slipped off when they were climbing trees in the garden,' said Jack. 'They keep *on* singing that silly song about us. I tried to remember the one that Colin made up about Binkie, but I couldn't. How does it go, Colin?'

But before Colin could tell him, someone came up to their door and rapped on it.

'Who's there?' called Peter. 'You can't come in unless you know the password. We're holding a meeting.'

'It's me, Matt the shepherd,' said a voice, and Peter opened the door at once. Matt stood there, looking rather cross.

'Have any of you been taking the clothes off that old scarecrow I dressed out in the field for your father?' he said. 'The crows are down there in their hundreds! They don't take fright at a turnip head and sticks – it's only when a scare-crow's dressed and looks like a man that they keep away.'

'No. No, of course we haven't taken the clothes!' said Peter, astonished. 'We wouldn't dream of it!'

'Well – you see if you can find out who did it!' said Matt. 'I'll have to tell your father about it this evening. You just find out for me, will you?' And away he tramped, leaving the Seven too astonished for words. Now, who would do a silly thing like that?

9 Crash!

The Secret Seven looked at each other in astonishment. 'Why, we saw the old scarecrow yesterday,' said Peter. 'There was a rook on his head – so
the birds can't be as scared of him as old Matt
said!'

'But who could have taken the clothes?' said
Jack. 'I mean – they were pretty old and torn,
weren't they?'

'Well, the scarecrow has worn them for a long
time,' said Janet. 'I wouldn't have thought they
were much good for *any*one!'

'They wouldn't be worth a single penny,' said
Peter. 'I must say I'm surprised at Matt thinking
we'd had anything to do with it!'

'Well, we did once do something silly with a
scarecrow,' said Janet. 'Don't you remember? We
planted some seeds in our own little gardens, and
when the birds came and pecked them up we
fetched an old scarecrow out of the wheat-field
and stood him in the middle of our own seeds!
Daddy was very cross – but Mother said we

hadn't meant any harm, we were too little then to understand.'

The others laughed at the picture of Janet and Peter dragging a scarecrow all the way to their own small gardens. 'All the same – I expect that's why Matt thought it was you,' said Colin.

'I suppose – I suppose it couldn't be Susie and Binkie, could it?' asked George.

Everyone thought it was very likely! 'It's just the silly sort of thing they *would* do,' said Jack. 'They would think it very, very funny – and they'd know we'd be questioned and feel really puzzled.'

'Well – you'd better ask Susie about it,' said Peter to Jack. 'And if she starts giggling and won't say anything, just say you'll report to *us* and we'll take the matter in hand, as we have been asked to find the clothes.'

'Yes. That sounds very official,' said Jack approvingly. 'I must say it would be a good idea if Colin finished his poem about Binkie, and even made one up about Susie. Those two want taking down a peg.'

'Well, to change the subject,' said Peter. 'Does anyone want to go to the cinema tonight? Janet and I are going, and we'd love to have some of the Secret Seven with us.'

'I can't come,' said Jack. 'If I ask about it, Mother will say that Susie and Binkie are to go too. And I'm *not* going to sit beside two giggly girls all evening.'

'And I can't come,' said Pam. 'Barbara and I are going out to tea with a friend.'

'I could come,' said Colin, and George nodded his head too. 'That would be four of us. We'll meet you at the cinema, five minutes before the film starts. What about the scarecrow clothes now? Do we bother to look about for them, or not?'

'Not till Jack has asked Susie and Binkie if they know anything,' said Peter, getting up. 'Well, that's the end of this meeting. I'll let you all know when there's another. I wish something exciting would happen – *not* like that horrid fire, though!'

That evening Janet and Peter met the other two at the cinema, paid for their tickets, and went in. It was a good film, and they all enjoyed it. They sat it out to the end and then left the cinema. It was a very dark night, with not a star to be seen.

Peter and Janet were on bicycles, but the other two were walking. 'Good-bye!' said the two cyclists and went off in the darkness, their lamps sending a wavering light in front of them.

Colin and George walked off slowly, talking as

they went. All the shops were shut, but some were still lighted, so that, although shut, their goods might still be displayed to any passer-by. The boys looked into them as they passed.

The bicycle shop was lighted up, and they stopped to admire the new racing bicycle in the middle of the window. The next lighted shop was an antique shop, which sold all kinds of interesting things – old pictures, ornaments, tea-sets, musical instruments, chairs, and other furniture.

The boys stopped to look at a picture of a long-ago battle, and then walked on again. At the corner Colin suddenly exclaimed, in panic, 'Hey – I believe I've lost my watch. Bother! I *shall* get into a row. Do you mind if we walk back and look for it, George? I might have dropped it in the cinema, of course.'

The boys turned and went back very slowly, George's torch lighting up the pavement, as they hunted for the watch. And then the torch flickered faintly – and went out, leaving them in black darkness.

'Look at that now – the battery's gone just when we needed the torch!' groaned Colin. 'Why didn't I bring mine as well? We can't look for the watch in this darkness, that's certain.'

Someone passed them, walking softly in the

road, not seeing the two boys standing still on the dark pavement, messing about with the useless torch. He passed so silently that the boys jumped.

'He walked as quietly as a policeman!' said George. 'Gosh – what about going after him, and if he *is* a policeman, we'll report the loss of your watch – then if anyone takes it to the police-station it will be returned to you at once – before you get into a row about it!'

'Good idea!' said Colin, and they went after the silent passer-by. They could just make him out in the distance as he passed a lighted shop.

They were almost up to him as he came near to the lighted antique shop, and were just about to call out to him, when he stopped and looked all round him in a curiously cautious manner.

'He's not a policeman after all,' said Colin. 'Hey – what's he doing?'

Things then happened very quickly indeed! The man took something from beneath his coat and threw it at the lighted window of the old antique shop!

CRASH!

The glass splintered at once, and fragments flew all about, glittering in the light from the shop window. The horrified boys saw the man snatch at something in the window and then race off with it at top speed.

He passed by them, and Colin put out a foot to stop him. But the man swerved and raced on, passing under a nearby lamp-post, and then disappearing into the night.

'After him!' shouted George, and they tore round the corner where the man had gone. But he was nowhere to be seen in the darkness – and certainly could not be heard for his tread had been absolutely silent.

What excitement there was then! The crash of breaking glass brought people flocking into the street, shouting and calling. A policeman appeared as if by magic – and someone ran out of the antique shop, joining in the clamour. Good gracious! Colin and George had certainly got something to tell the Secret Seven!

10   Very surprising

Colin and George ran up to the antique shop. The little man who owned it was wringing his hands as he saw his smashed windows, and everything inside covered with broken glass.

'What's all this?' said the big policeman, looming up silently, and taking out a notebook. 'Who did this?'

'A man,' said someone. 'I just caught sight of him across the road. I couldn't tell you what he was like, though. He raced off at once.'

'What's been taken, sir?' said the policeman to the shopkeeper.

'Oh, that I can't say till I've had a good look,' said the man. 'My word – that picture's done for – that battle picture. The flying glass has cut it to bits – and the brick has smashed that lovely old vase. I don't rightly know what was in the window, sir, till I ask my assistant. He did the window for me yesterday, when I was away. Oh my word, what a mess!'

There was quite a crowd now, round the shop,

and soon another policeman came. Colin and George wondered if they ought to say that they, too, had seen the man smash the window, and were just screwing up their courage to do so, when one of the policemen saw that there were a few children in the crowd.

'You get off home,' he said sternly. 'Go on now. You can't help us, you only hinder us. Clear off!'

Colin and George slipped away at once. They had seen all they wanted to, and they were pretty sure that they couldn't give much help. Also, they didn't much like the thought of being stared at by so many people if they went up to the policemen and spoke to them. Why, some of them might think that they had smashed the window, and were owning up!

We MUST get Peter to call a meeting tomorrow and tell the Secret Seven about this,' panted George as they ran home. 'I don't expect we can *do* anything. But I think we *ought* to tell the others.'

Colin agreed. Anyway, it would be most exciting to relate the story to them! How he wished he and George had managed to trip the man up, and perhaps catch him. What a thrill *that* would have been!

Colin telephoned to Peter the next morning. 'Peter – is that you? Listen, George and I saw a thief smash a window coming home from the cinema last night and steal something out of the antique shop. We actually *saw* the man. Do you think we could have a meeting about it? It's really very exciting.'

'Gosh – did you actually *see* him?' said Peter. 'Dad heard about it from his cowman, and told us at breakfast – and Janet and I groaned because we thought we'd been just too early to see it happen.'

'Well, we had to go back to see if we could find my watch,' said Colin. 'If we hadn't done that we'd have missed all the excitement. What time shall we come to the meeting, Peter? George and I can go round and tell the others now, if you like.'

'Right. Well, bring them along as soon as possible,' said Peter. 'Janet and I will be waiting down in the shed.'

It was quite an excited group of children who met in the shed some time later. All of them had heard of the smashing of the window, but nobody except Pam knew what had been stolen.

She listened quietly to the story told by Colin and George, as did the others. Peter and Janet wished that Colin had discovered that his watch was missing before he had said good-bye to them – then they, too, would have seen the excitement.

'Actually,' said Colin, 'I *hadn't* lost my watch,

after all! I found it on my dressing-table when I got home!'

'*Did* you?' said George. 'Gosh – and to think how we searched every inch of the pavement! By the way, does anyone know if the man has been caught yet?'

'Not so far,' said Peter. 'My father had to see the police this morning about a dog that's worrying our sheep – and the policeman told him they hadn't the foggiest idea who the thief was – or why the man wanted to steal anything from the antique shop. Dad didn't hear what was stolen, however. Does anyone know?'

'Yes, *I* know,' said Pam at once. 'It was a very, very old violin, worth thousands of pounds! It was in the very front of the window, with a card telling its history. The man took that, and the bow too!'

'Ah – he must be a violinist, then,' said Peter, saying what everyone was thinking. 'They'll be checking on all the local violinists, I expect.'

'I hope they won't question Miss Hilbrun, the violin teacher at our school!' said Pam. 'She's a wonderful player – but I'm sure she would go into a dead faint if a policeman wanted to ask her questions. She even had to go and sit down for half an hour once, in the middle of teaching, because someone let the piano-lid drop with a bang!'

'I bet you were the one that did that,' said Jack.

'I was not. It was your sister Susie,' said Pam. 'You might have guessed that! Oh dear – it really makes me smile to think of our mouse-like Miss Hilbrun throwing a brick into a window to steal a violin!'

'Listen, George and Colin,' said Peter. 'According to the policeman Dad spoke to this morning when he was reporting that dog, nobody seemed to know exactly how the man was dressed or what he looked like. Did *you* happen to notice? You ought to have done, because that's one of the rules of the Secret Seven – always to be observant, and keep our eyes open.'

'Well – yes – I think I can tell you more or less what he looked like,' said George, though Colin looked rather blank. 'I can't say that I actually noted it all – but I did get a very good view of him in the bright light from the window, just as he smashed it – a sort of quick photograph of him in my mind, if you know what I mean.'

'Tell us, then,' said Peter, taking out his notebook. 'It might be really useful. We could look out for him if we know, for instance, what he's wearing.'

'Well – he was medium size,' said George, half-shutting his eyes to picture the man in his mind. 'And he had a very torn old coat of brown tweed – *very* torn. And trousers that were a kind of light grey and very dirty. And a black hat with a hole in it. And, oh yes – a scarf round his neck with red-and-white spots.'

Peter gave a loud exclamation. 'George! Do you know what you've just described EXACTLY? The clothes that were stolen from the *scarecrow*!'

11 A very interesting meeting

The Secret Seven stared at Peter in the utmost amazement. What! The violin thief had been dressed in the clothes stolen from the scarecrow? But WHY?

'You don't suppose it was the *scarecrow* who stole out in the night and took the violin, do you?' said Pam, with one of her sudden giggles.

'Don't be silly. You know the scarecrow hasn't any clothes now – unless Matt has found some more for him,' said Janet.

'This is very, very interesting,' said Peter slowly. 'It certainly rules out jokers like Susie or Binkie.'

'Well, I *did* ask them,' said Jack, 'and honestly I couldn't make out whether they knew anything about the scarecrow's clothes or not, they giggled so. I half thought they *did*, as a matter of fact.'

'Well, they couldn't have. They were just pulling your leg,' said Peter. 'Now let's think carefully about this, and if anyone has a sensible remark, please make it. We know two things –

one, that a man stole a very valuable old violin last night – and two, that for some reason he wore old clothes belonging to a scarecrow. Now what do we make of that?'

'Well, if the violin was old and valuable, and was obviously the one thing he had made up his mind to steal, it's clear that he must have been a violinist himself, or know about the value of old ones,' said Colin at once. 'The odds are that he is a musician, if not a violinist.'

'And he wore those awful old clothes as a disguise so that if he were seen he couldn't possibly be recognised,' said Barbara.

'And he didn't want to buy them at an old clothes shop or borrow them from any tramp, in case of questions being asked,' said Jack.

'So he spotted our scarecrow and took the clothes from *him*!' said Peter. 'And presumably he will throw them away now or hide them somewhere.'

'He might put them on the scarecrow again,' suggested George.

'No. He'd be afraid that it might be watched,' said Peter. 'Anyway, it's sure to be dressed up again now. No – he'll either burn or bury those clothes.'

'We could look for them – only we'd probably

never find them!' said Janet. 'I mean – there's the whole countryside to hide them in!'

'Yes, that's true,' said Peter. 'Well – has anyone any other suggestion?'

Nobody had. It seemed impossible to hunt for a violinist they didn't know who had been dressed in clothes he had probably already hidden away!

'Do we know any first-class violinists who would love a valuable old violin?' asked Pam hopefully.

'Well, yes we do,' said Peter, 'but none of them would dress up in scarecrow clothes and smash a shop-window. I mean, there's old Mr Scraper at school, who teaches the violin – but I can't possibly imagine him doing things like that. Or Mr Luton, our churchwarden – he plays the violin too, so does his wife. But they wouldn't go about smashing windows. No – it must be someone a bit mad, I think, who has an urge to steal and use a really precious old violin.'

'But yet sensible enough to use the scarecrow's clothes as a disguise!' said Jack.

'Yes. Well, it's a puzzle. I don't really see that there's anything we can do to solve it at the moment,' said Peter. 'Except look out for old clothes stuffed in a ditch or a bush, or buried somewhere.'

Scamper suddenly began to bark loudly, and everyone looked up. 'I bet that's Susie,' said Jack, in disgust. 'We've got to go and see my granny this morning, and Susie said she'd call for me here. I *told* her not to! Interrupting our meeting!'

The rude Secret Seven song came on the air at that moment, sung lustily by two voices – Susie's and Binkie's.

> 'Oh see the Secret Seven,
>   So very smug and pi,
>   Eyes turned up to Heaven,
>   When they come walking by!
>   They think . . .'

Colin flew to the door and opened it. He sang at the top of *his* voice – and he had a really loud one –

> 'Oh Binkie has the habit
>   Of a silly little rabbit,
>   Twitching up and down her little nose!
>   And in her mouth beneath
>   Are lots of rabbit teeth
>   And that's the way a little Binkie grows!'

The Secret Seven listened in delight. That would serve Binkie right for making up such a horrid poem about *them*! They hadn't heard the end of the poem before, because Colin had only thought of it that very minute!

Susie marched right up to Colin, red in the face with anger.

'You've made Binkie cry with that song!' she said. 'How dare you? I'll pay you back, you Secret Seven, for making up such an unkind song about my best friend.'

'Well, Binkie started it, with her rude Secret Seven song,' said Colin stoutly. But all the same he felt rather ashamed of making Binkie cry. Perhaps it *was* rather an unkind song.

'Jack, you're to come now,' ordered Susie. 'Granny will be waiting for us.'

'All right, all right. Don't order me about,' said Jack. He turned to the others. 'What about this afternoon?' he said. 'Are we going anywhere?'

'We might go up and have a look to see how the gingerbread woman, Mrs Bolan, is getting on in her caravan,' said Peter. 'Mother has given us some baby clothes to take up, and I thought I'd take my old toy bus for Benny.'

'Right. I'll be along about half-past two. Is that all right?' asked Jack.

'Make it three,' said Peter, and the others

nodded. 'We'll keep an eye open for scarecrow clothes on the way,' he added, lowering his voice.

'*I* heard you,' said Susie, at once. 'And what's more, I know you and the others think that Binkie and I were the idiots who took the scarecrow clothes, but we didn't. Jack asked us about them. It's just about time you Secret Seven made a mistake about something! You think you're too clever for words. So look out – else you'll be sorry!' And away she went with Binkie.

'Now what exactly does she mean by *that*?' said Peter.

12 Scamper makes a find

At about three o'clock that afternoon the Secret Seven set off through the fields to go to visit the Bolans' caravan. Scamper raced along with them as usual.

'We shall pass the scarecrow on the way,' said Colin. 'I wonder what he's wearing now?'

He was fully dressed again, in a curious collection of clothes. He wore a woman's hat with a feather in – a raincoat full of holes, and old macintosh trousers, very torn. He stood there looking rather forlorn and ashamed of himself.

Janet gave a squeal of laughter when she saw his hat.

'That's the hat that the cowman's wife used to wear in church!' she said. 'I've often and often watched that feather waggling in it when she fell asleep on a hot Sunday!'

'And those trousers belong to the cowman,' said Peter. 'He must have got a new pair. I think the macintosh is the shepherd's. Well – the old scarecrow looks peculiar now, doesn't he? Hi, Scarecrow! Where are your other clothes?'

The scarecrow flapped his sleeves dismally and didn't answer! They left him standing sadly in the field, and went on towards the Bolans' caravan, up by Matt the shepherd's hut.

On the way they had to pass over a small bridge across a gurgling stream. Scamper, hearing the water, ran joyfully ahead. Now he could get a drink!

But he stopped before he came to the little stream and began to sniff in a ditch in the greatest excitement.

'What's up, Scamper?' called Peter. 'What are you scrabbling at?'

Scamper was certainly excited. He barked, and scraped vigorously with his front paws. The Secret Seven came up to him and looked down in amusement. Then Janet gave a little cry.

'Peter! Look – what's that sticking out of the hole he's made? It looks like a bit of cloth. Oh, PETER! It couldn't be the scarecrow clothes, could it?'

'Well – this does look a bit like old grey flannel – and we know that the scarecrow's trousers *were* flannels!' said Peter, feeling a little surge of excitement welling up inside him. 'Go on, Scamper. Find it, then, find it!'

Scamper scraped at top speed, flinging out earth behind him, and covering the Seven with it. Soon he had got firm hold of whatever was there, and tugged it right out in triumph.

'Wuff!' he said. 'Wuff, wuff, wuff!'

Peter picked up the piece of grey flannel. It didn't look like trousers. It looked more like a torn piece of skirt. He looked down at Scamper, who was busy burrowing again in the hole he had made, giving little whines of excitement.

'He's got something else there,' said Jack. 'Maybe the old hat.'

Yes – in half a minute Scamper brought up an old hat – but what a hat! It was a very old straw one, with a ribbon round it – a ribbon that Pam recognised only too well!

'Peter! That's one of our old school hats and the school ribbon we wear at our school! This hat has never been on any scarecrow! Whatever does it all mean?'

'Wuff!' said Scamper again, in delight, and put his nose right into the hole he had made. He brought out a large and extremely smelly bone, which he proudly laid at Peter's feet.

'Good gracious!' said Peter, amazed. 'So that's

why you dug down there – you smelt the bone! But why in the world did anyone bury the . . .'

And just then there came the sound of someone exploding into laughter. What an explosion that was! The Seven turned at once – and there were Susie and Binkie, rolling about on a bank of grass, behind which they had been spying on the excited Seven!

'Oh, I'll die of laughing! Oh, I can't bear it! Oh Scamper, you're a perfect wonder! Oh, I've got such a stitch in my side!'

That was Susie, of course. She went off into a cascade of laughs again, and Binkie joined her, shouting out just like Susie.

'Oh did you see their faces when they found your old school hat, Susie? Oh, I'm dying of laughing! I can't laugh any more, I'm crying with laughter! Oh, that smelly old bone! Good old Scamper!'

Scamper couldn't make out why Susie and Binkie were rolling about and squealing. He thought they must be hurt, and he put his tail down and ran over to them, whining.

'Come back, Scamper,' said Peter, and Scamper ran back, surprised at Peter's stern voice.

'I suppose you think this is funny,' began Peter, calling to the two girls. 'Well . . .'

'Oh yes, we do think it's funny!' laughed Susie, wiping her eyes. 'The funniest thing that ever happened. You were all so solemn!'

'Oh come on – let's leave them to their silly giggling,' said Jack furiously, and the Seven walked with great dignity to the little stream and crossed the bridge. But after a little while Pam gave a sudden giggle. She looked round apologetically.

'Sorry,' she said. 'But honestly it *was* rather funny.' And she gave another little giggle.

Barbara couldn't help joining in. 'We must have looked funny, poring over a bit of Susie's old school skirt and her old school hat,' she said, and began to laugh.

And then, of course, everyone saw the funny side, and they roared with laughter, just as Susie and Binkie had. Oh dear – how easily they had been taken in!

'It was really rather clever of them to think of burying the bone at the *bottom* of the hole, and putting the other things on top,' said Janet. 'I mean – they must have planned it very well, really. They knew we were coming up here . . .'

'And that old Scamper would smell the bone, and scrape a hole,' said Jack. 'And that we'd get all excited to see the piece of cloth there. Oh dear –

we were properly taken in. Well, they've paid us back all right.'

'Here we are, almost at the caravan,' said Peter. 'And there's Mrs Bolan, look, doing some washing outside. Hallo, Mrs Bolan!'

13   An odd little boy

Mrs Bolan looked up as the children came towards her.

'Well, it's nice to see you,' she said, smiling her nice smile. 'Oh – what's that you've brought me? What a lovely little coat – and a little dress too. The baby won't know herself!'

'And I brought this for Benny,' said Peter, producing the bus. 'Where is he?'

'Somewhere about,' said his mother, and called: 'Benny! Where are you, love? Benny, there's a present for you.'

But no Benny appeared. 'He's hiding,' said his mother. 'He's scared of visitors.'

'Doesn't he go to school?' asked Pam, looking all round for the little boy. 'Or is he too young?'

'He's eight,' said Mrs Bolan. 'He's never been to school. He wouldn't like it, and it wouldn't be any good. Poor Benny – he hasn't had much luck in his life. Oh land's sake, look at that baby now, hanging half out of her pram! What I'll do with her when she can walk, I *don't* know. But there, maybe Benny will look after her – he loves his little sister.'

The girls wandered off to look inside the caravan. It looked cosy and comfortable, but not very tidy or very clean.

'Did we give you everything you needed?' asked Janet. 'We tried to think of everything.'

'Yes, love – all except needles and cottons!' said Mrs Bolan, laughing. 'You wouldn't believe how much I've wanted those – to run up little curtains for the windows, and to mend my clothes – these I stand in are the only ones I've got – all the others were burnt.'

'Oh – we never even thought of needles and cottons – or scissors either,' said Janet. 'I expect you wanted scissors too didn't you, Mrs Bolan?'

'Oh yes – but Luke left me his penknife,' said Mrs Bolan, squeezing out her washing. 'And Matt the shepherd is good to me – he brings me other little things, you know.'

'We'll come up again as soon as we can, Mrs Bolan,' promised Janet, 'and bring you a small work-basket. I never use my old one; you can have that. Is there anything else?'

'Well, I suppose you haven't an old bucket to spare, have you?' asked Mrs Bolan. 'You did bring one, but Benny's gone off with it, bless his heart. He plays little tunes on it with a stick – he's clever at that, and it keeps him happy, poor lamb.'

'Yes, we'll bring you a bucket too,' said Peter. 'As soon as we can. Listen – what's that noise?'

'Oh, that's Benny with his bucket!' said Mrs Bolan. 'Sounds quite like music, doesn't it! Dinga-dinga-dong-dong, dinga-dinga-dong, dong! Benny, you bring me my bucket!'

There was silence after that, and Mrs Bolan shook her head. 'No good going after him,' she said. 'He'll hide himself somewhere, and keep as still as a rabbit in its burrow.'

'Is your husband still down at the fair?' asked Peter.

'The fair's moved on,' she answered. 'Didn't you know? Luke's gone with it. It moved off this morning, and Luke won't be back with me for a few days. I shall miss him, up here alone on the hills. But old Matt there, he keeps coming to see if I'm all right!'

Janet thought she was a brave, cheerful, and generous little woman. She remembered how she had given them a batch of her hot gingerbread at the fair, when they had no money to pay for it.

'There's Benny!' said Jack suddenly, and beckoned to the small boy, who took no notice at all. He had appeared beside some gorse bushes, and stood staring across at them, scarcely blinking his great dark eyes.

'There now – you see he's hidden that bucket of mine somewhere, just as I said!' said Mrs Bolan. 'Benny, you come over here. There's a lovely present for you, a beauty. It's a bus! You come and get it.'

Benny stood quite silent, still staring. The children thought him a very odd little boy indeed, but he was a striking and lovely child, and Janet longed to give him a hug. He began to walk over to them, slowly and carefully, as if afraid of falling. He stopped fairly near and stared towards them again.

Peter went over to him with the bus. He held it out, but the child made no attempt to take it. So Peter put it gently into his hands, and at once the boy clutched it, and ran his fingers all over it in delight.

When he found the little hooter that said 'Toot-toot!' his whole face lit up and he smiled sweetly.

'Toot-toot-toot!' he sang, in a tuneful little voice. 'It's a bus, Mammy, a bus. Is it for me, Mammy?'

'Yes, for you,' said his mother. 'Say thank you nicely to Peter.'

'Thank you,' said Benny, looking at George,

instead of at Peter. Janet thought he had the strangest eyes she had ever seen, dark, beautiful, and deep, but without any expression at all.

Scamper ran up and pushed his head against Benny's leg. Benny backed away, half scared, and Peter called Scamper to him. Benny went off to the bushes, carrying his precious bus.

'Goo!' said the baby, bouncing up and down in her pram. 'Goo-goo!' She wanted attention too, and Janet went over to her at once. She was as lively as Benny was quiet. She put her fat little hand against Janet's cheek.

'She likes you,' said Mrs Bolan, smiling. 'Now stop bouncing, you little monkey, or you'll have the springs out of that old pram!'

'It's time to go,' said Peter, looking at his watch. 'Mrs Bolan, we'll bring you a bucket, and needles and cotton and any other little thing we can think of as soon as we can! I'm so glad you like the caravan.'

'Oh, it's fine,' said Mrs Bolan cheerfully. She was now pegging up clothes on a line that stretched from one tree to another. 'Thank you for coming.'

The Seven went off together, with Scamper trotting in front, sniffing at everything. When he came to the hole where the bone had been he remembered that he had left his precious, magnificent bone up at the caravan site, and bounded back to fetch it.

'Well, I'm glad we went up there,' said Janet. 'But Benny puzzles me. What a strange little boy – and I really do think he ought to go to school. He's eight! I'll tell Mother about him, and perhaps she can arrange something.'

'Here comes Scamper again,' said Peter. 'Pooh, take that bone away from me, Scamper – it's the smelliest, nastiest one I've ever known!'

14 Something very strange

Two days went by, and the Seven were very busy with all kinds of things. Peter and Janet lime-washed the hen-houses for their father, with Scamper watching in great interest.

'You look a bit peculiar, Scamper – splashed with white from the lime-wash drips,' said Janet. 'Why *must* you sit exactly under where we're working – you get all the splashes!'

George was busy too, with Colin, rigging a fine ship they had made together. Jack was helping at home. The two girls, Pam and Barbara, were earning a little money by weeding onion beds.

'Horrible job!' Pam told Peter, when she saw him. 'The weeds *will* grow all tangled up with the onion stems, and we keep pulling up tiny onions with the weeds, and have to replant them! Still – we earn fifty pence an hour!'

They often spoke about the stolen violin, especially Colin and George, who spent a good deal of time together on the ship. It was they who had seen the window being smashed, of course, and it was interesting to talk about such an exciting happening.

'It rather looks as if this business about the stolen violin is fading out,' Colin said to George. 'My father asked the police if they'd heard anything about it, or had an idea of who the thief was, but they hadn't.'

'Well, they won't now,' said George. 'The man's gone off with it. I expect he's a hundred miles away!'

Peter and Janet finished their job in the henhouses, and decided to take a day off.

'We think we'll go for a walk, Mother,' said Peter. 'May we have sandwiches?'

'Yes, dear. I'll make you some,' said his mother. 'If you're going near old Matt the shepherd, take him this letter, will you? It didn't come till after he'd fetched his milk this morning.'

'Right,' said Peter. 'We'll go to the woods, I think, and see how far the bluebells are up, and have our picnic there – and then we'll go home over the hill where Matt has his sheep.'

'And we'll look in on the Bolans,' said Janet. 'I love that little baby. Oh Mother, can you give me an old pair of scissors, please? I promised Mrs Bolan I'd take her a pair, and some needles too. You did send a bucket up by Matt, didn't you?'

'No. Matt said she could borrow his,' said Mother. 'Anyhow till that monkey of a boy brings back the bucket we sent before.'

'He's not a monkey at all,' said Janet, remembering the big-eyed, solemn little boy. 'He's a strange little fellow. He only took the bucket to play tunes on!'

The children set off with their sandwiches, Scamper running joyfully ahead. It was a wonderful day again, and the sun was as hot as June. Primroses nestled everywhere, and little wild anemones danced gaily in shady corners. Janet skipped along happily.

'It's lovely to have a day all to ourselves after sticking to that lime-washing job for hour after hour,' she said. 'I wonder if any bluebells will be out. It's terribly early, but you never know.'

The woods were full of springing bluebell leaves, their long green spikes standing guard over the flowers pushing up between them. Janet found one flower right out, its bells a lovely blue.

'Here's one! And another! Oh, I wish we could find a white one. That's so very, very lucky!'

'Better not pick any,' said Peter. 'They would only be dead by the time we get home!'

They had their lunch in the bluebell wood, with the blackbirds and thrushes singing loudly overhead, and a little robin hopping round their feet, waiting for a crumb. Then they went on again, climbing the hills to where Matt the shepherd kept his sheep.

He wasn't in his hut, so they left his letter there, and then went across to where the Bolans had their caravan, a little way off. But that was shut too, and no one was about, not even Benny.

'The sheep are on the opposite hill today,' said Peter, sitting down on the grass. 'What a lot Dad's got now, hasn't he? And how the lambs have grown!'

'It must be rather nice to be a shepherd up on the hills, living by himself with the sheep and the lambs he loves,' said Janet, sitting down beside him. 'Oh look – isn't that old Matt coming up the path over there? And his dog too!'

It was. He smiled when he saw them, and his eyes shone as blue as the sky. Janet wondered why so many people who lived in the open air had such very blue eyes. She ran to meet the old shepherd.

'Well, Janet, it's nice to see you and your dog,' said Matt, leaning on his big crook. 'It isn't often old Matt has visitors. Me and my dog here, we don't see much company.'

'What about the Bolans? You see them, don't you?' asked Peter.

'Oh yes – and Mrs Bolan is a right kind woman,' said Matt. 'I haven't seen her husband. He comes home at odd times, mostly late at night. He works in the fairs, you know. But that boy Benny – he's a strange little fellow, now. Sits and stares at nothing for hours! It's my belief he's not right in the head.'

'Oh dear!' said Janet. 'Perhaps that's why he doesn't go to school, then. Poor little boy.'

'I'd like to set him on my knee and tell him a tale,' said Matt. 'But as soon as he hears anyone coming he's off like a frightened rabbit. I'm wondering if he was scared last night, if he heard what I heard?'

'Why? What did you hear?' asked Peter, in surprise.

'I don't rightly know, Peter,' said Matt, screwing up his wrinkled forehead. 'I was in my hut, half asleep, when I heard it. It was about half-past nine, and a dark night too! What a wailing it was! What a sad, sad noise! It rose up and down, up and down, till I couldn't bear it and went out on the hillside to see if some animal was in pain – and yet it sounded like no living thing. But there was nothing there. As soon as I called out, the wailing stopped.'

Peter and Janet listened in astonishment. What a

weird tale! Wailing? Who would be wailing? And why?

'The noise went high and it went low,' said Matt. 'I never did hear such wailing before. It fair went through me, and gripped my heart. I was really glad when it stopped!'

'Do you think it will come tonight?' asked Peter. Matt shook his head.

'How do I know? Maybe – and maybe not. I asked Mrs Bolan about it this morning, and she said she hadn't heard anything. But it was wailing all right!'

'Janet, I'm going to get Jack to come up here and listen with me tonight!' said Peter, as Matt got up to fetch his pipe. 'Wailing! That's something very odd. We'll find out what it is!'

15 Up on the hills at night

Peter and Janet longed to tell the others this new, strange piece of news. They raced down the hill, with Scamper at their heels.

They passed Jack's house on the way and called in to see him. He was having a jigsaw competition with Susie and Binkie, who at once began to chant the Secret Seven song under their breath. Most annoying!

'Jack, can you spare a moment?' asked Peter. 'We've some rather strange news.'

'What is it?' asked Susie at once, her quick, bird-like eyes staring brightly at Peter.

'I'm afraid it's Secret Seven news,' said Peter coldly. 'Can you come, Jack? You can finish your jigsaw afterwards.'

'Yes, of course,' said Jack, and got up. 'Back in a few minutes,' he said to Susie and Binkie and marched out with Peter and Janet.

'I'm glad you came,' he said, taking them into another room. 'Mother has made me play with those two girls all day. Oooh – girls! What a bore they are.'

'Thank you very much, Jack,' said Janet indignantly. 'Perhaps I'd better go, and leave you with Peter.'

'No. No, of course not!' said Jack, in alarm. 'I didn't mean *you*. You're fine. It's just those two that get on my nerves.'

Peter snorted. 'Idiots,' he said. 'They must lead you an awful life, Jack. But listen, I want you to do something with me tonight. It's not exactly to do with anything the Secret Seven have been working on, but it's rather strange.'

He told Jack what Matt had said. Jack was amazed. 'He must have been dreaming, don't you think?' he said. 'I mean – what would go wailing out on those hills? If it was an animal, caught in a trap or something, poor thing, old Matt would recognise its wail or howl. If it's something he couldn't place he *must* have been dreaming!'

'I didn't think of that,' said Peter. 'Of course, it might have been a dream – but he said he got up and went out of his hut and still heard it. It stopped when he called out, though.'

'When he woke up, I expect!' said Jack, with a grin.

'Well – perhaps it's not worth bothering about,' said Peter, rather downcast.

'I think it is – and if you don't go, I shall get

Pam and Barbara, and we'll go,' said Janet un-expectedly.

The two boys looked at her in surprise.

'No,' said Jack at once. 'It's not right for girls to go by themselves up on the hills at night. I'll go with Peter, of course I will. Shall we ask Colin and George, Peter?'

'Yes. We'll make a sort of adventure of it,' said Peter, pleased. Then, as Janet opened her mouth to argue, he frowned. 'And don't you start asking if you and the other two girls can come, Janet, because you CAN'T!'

'All right, all right,' said Janet, looking rather sulky. How very annoying to be kept out of so many exciting things!

The boys quickly arranged everything. Jack said he would go round and tell Colin and George, and they would all be outside Peter's front gate as soon as it was dark.

'Bring torches, for goodness' sake,' said Peter. 'There's no moon, and if it's a cloudy night it will be as dark as pitch.'

'Come on – we'd better get back home,' said Janet, looking at her watch. 'We're late for tea already.'

They went quickly out of the room – and heard a stifled giggle. They stopped indignantly.

'Have those two girls been listening?' demanded Peter. 'We shut the door. Surely they
aren't mean enough to listen through the key-
hole?'

'Susie and Binkie would do *any*thing,' said Jack
desperately, and raced after the giggles that could
still be heard in the distance.

Peter was very cross, and so was Janet. Why
ever hadn't they gone into a corner of the garden,
where nobody could possibly hear a word? Well,
the only blessing was that they had spoken in
fairly low voices, so perhaps Susie and Binkie
hadn't heard anything much.

Jack went round to tell Colin and George, and
to see if they would like to join in the little
adventure. They both laughed at the 'wailing' old
Matt had heard, but said they would certainly
come.

'We *were* going to the cinema tonight, but
we'll come with you and Peter instead,' said
Colin.

'Half-past seven outside Peter's front gate,' said
Jack. 'No bikes. We'll have to walk up those hills –
and let's hope the scarecrow doesn't chase us
when we pass his field!'

'It was a funny business about his clothes,
wasn't it?' said Colin. 'We never found out

anything about those – they just vanished. Right, Jack – you can count on us.'

So, when it was nice and dark, the four boys met outside Peter's gate. Janet was there too, to see them off. 'I *wish* I could come,' she said, still hopeful that she might. But it was no good! The boys said good-bye and strode off up the dark lane, leaving poor Scamper behind too.

It took them some time to get to where old Matt had his hut.

'We won't let him know we're here, in case he's cross about it,' said Peter, in a low voice. 'I vote we sit down behind this bush. I wonder if Matt is in his hut.'

'Yes. I can see a crack of light,' said George. 'He's there all right. Now, we'd better sit absolutely still and quiet, so that the wailer won't guess we're listening or watching.'

So the four boys sat there in utter silence, jumping once when an owl gave a sudden hoot, and straining their ears when some small creature ran over the grass.

And then suddenly the wailing began! Good gracious! What a horrible noise! Wooooooo-ooh! Waaaaa-ah! Eeeeeeeeeee! The boys clutched one another, their hearts thumping violently.

'It sounds right behind our bush!' whispered

Peter. 'Let's creep round and shine our torches!'

'Woooooo-oooh! Waaaaa-ah! Eeeeeeeee!'

'Now – quick!' said Peter, and round the bush they went.

16 The strange wailing

The four boys switched on their torches as they stumbled round the great gorse bush – and almost before they got there, they heard another noise – *not* a wail – which filled them with surprise and anger.

They shone their torches on two figures crouching there, both holding their sides with laughter.

'Susie! Binkie! You beasts!' cried Jack, in horror and anger. 'You listened to what Peter said this morning. You've spoilt EVERYTHING!'

'Was our wailing good?' asked Susie, half-choking with laughter. 'Did old Matt hear us too? And the Bolans? We call ourselves the Weird and Wonderful Wailers – did you know?'

A tall figure suddenly looked up in the light of the four torches. It was Matt the shepherd.

'What's this?' he said sternly. 'What are you children doing here at this time of night? What was all that yelling?'

'It wasn't yelling – it was Binkie and I wailing,'

said Susie. 'Didn't you hear it last night, Matt?'

'What I heard last night wasn't made by any silly child,' said Matt solemnly. 'You be off before the *real* wailing starts. Yes, all of you. And you, Susie, I'll tell your father of you, so I will. Coming up here in the dark of night!'

'Oh no – please don't tell Dad,' said Susie, really alarmed, and got up in a hurry.

'Come on, Susie,' said Binkie, feeling scared by the stern shepherd. 'Quick!'

And she ran off down the hillside, shining her torch in front of her, Susie following close behind. Jack went after them. 'Wait for me, you idiots. You'll get lost. SUSIE! Wait for me! I'll take you home.'

'You be off too, lads,' said Matt, to the other three. 'If you should hear what *I* heard, you'll be tearing down the hill as if a hundred dogs were after you. Now go. Good night to you.'

And with great dignity the old man walked back to his shack. The boys heard the door shut. They switched off their torches, feeling angry and uncomfortable.

'That Susie!' said George. 'Horrible girl! And Binkie too. Coming up here like that! I must say you were an idiot Peter, to let Susie overhear what you told Jack.'

'Yes. But honestly you don't expect people to listen at keyholes,' said Peter. 'Though Susie will do anything, of course, to make fun of the Secret Seven. That's all she does it for.'

'Well, shall we push off home too?' asked Colin. 'I must say this is all very disappointing.'

'We'll wait just a bit – in case the real wailing, that Matt told us about, does happen to come again,' said Peter. 'He said he thought it came about half-past eight – and it's gone that now.'

'Well – five more minutes, then,' said Colin. 'But I'm pretty certain old Matt dreamt it all.'

They sat silently for five minutes, in the pitch-black darkness. Not a star was to be seen in the overclouded sky. An owl hooted again, and the wind made tiny noises in the gorse-bush behind them. Then a bird in a nearby bush unexpectedly gave a little chirrup and was silent again.

'Better go now,' whispered Peter, and rose to his feet. The others stood up too, and Peter took a few steps forward.

Then he stopped very suddenly indeed, and so did the others. Their hearts began to beat fast again, and Colin clutched hold of George.

A strange, sad wailing came on the air – oh how strange and how sad! It rose up through the night, high and full of beauty, and then fell again to a lower note, mournful but still pure and lovely.

Not a sound was to be heard except that strange, unearthly noise. Even the wind seemed to be listening, holding its breath, as were all three boys. They stood transfixed, clutching one another, not making any other movement.

They heard Matt's door open. The old shepherd must have heard the wailing too. It wasn't a dream of his. It was real!

There it was again, filling the night with mournfulness, and yet with beauty too – what a strange, strange sound to hear up on the lonely hillside.

'What is it?' whispered Colin at last.

'Don't you know?' said Peter. 'It's someone playing a violin! That's all it is. But oh, what wonderful playing! No tune. Just playing like the wind plays, or the trees, going on and on and on!'

'A violin!' said George. 'Of course! But I've never heard one played quite like that before. Who's playing it? And why, out on this hill in the dark night?'

Then they heard Matt's voice, stern and clear in the darkness.

'Who are you? Come forth and show yourself!'

The sounds stopped at once, and not another note was heard. Matt stood at his door for a few minutes and then went inside his hut. The boys heard the door shut.

'Sit down here,' said Peter, in a low, excited voice. 'I want to say something.' They all sat down, and in the darkness Peter spoke urgently.

'That violin! It must be the one that was stolen! I've never heard a violin played like that before – the notes were so pure and so lovely. And to think that Matt called it wailing!'

'Well – it *was* a kind of wailing – violin music often does wail,' said Colin. 'But it was beautiful. Yes – I bet it was the stolen violin. But who was playing it?'

'Luke Bolan!' said Peter promptly.

'How do you know?' asked George.

'Well – we know he plays the banjo, so he may be able to play the violin too,' said Peter. 'And his banjo was burnt in the fire – so maybe he stole that violin to make up for it.'

There was a silence after this. Then Peter spoke again. 'The next thing for us to do is to find the violin – he probably hides it in his caravan,' he said. 'Let's go quietly over to it now, and see if there's a light inside. Better be very careful, because if Luke was playing it on the hillside, he may still be out there. No torches on, please!'

The three boys crept over towards the caravan. Would they see Luke inside, with the violin? The *stolen* violin?

17 Where is the violin?

At first the three boys could not see the caravan at all, the night was so dark. They stumbled forward as quietly as they could, holding out their hands in front of them.

'Sh!' said Peter suddenly and stopped. The others bumped into him. 'Look!' whispered Peter. 'You can just see the outline of the caravan against the dark sky. Isn't that it?'

'Yes,' whispered back Colin. 'But there's no one there – it's quite dark.'

'Strange!' said Peter. 'Well – let's go as close as we can. Stop if you hear the slightest noise.'

They crept right up to the silent caravan. Not a chink of light was to be seen. Peter crept up the steps and listened. Ah – there *was* a sound inside! But what was it?

'It's someone crying!' said Colin. Yes – there was someone sobbing quietly, like a child!

'It must be little Benny, left all alone in the van,' said Peter. 'Is the pram anywhere about?' He switched on his torch to see. But it was not in its usual place beside the caravan, and was nowhere to be seen. The sobbing still went on inside the van.

Then a voice made them jump almost out of their skins. It was old Matt again! He must have seen their torches and come over from his shack.

'Didn't I tell you lads to clear off home?' he said. 'Peter, does your father know you're out? And what are you doing on the steps of that caravan?'

'Matt – that wailing – it was someone playing a violin!' said Peter.

Matt stood silent a moment. Then he spoke in a voice of wonder. 'I think you're right! But I've never heard a fiddle played like that before. A-wailing and a-woe-ing! Who played it? There's no one in the Bolans' caravan, except young Benny tonight, that I do know for the Bolans asked me to keep an eye on it, while they went down to see someone about a cottage.'

'Oh – then it's poor little Benny crying in there because he's frightened of the wailing too!' said Peter. 'Shall we go in and comfort him?'

'No. He's afraid of people,' said the shepherd. 'But he's not afraid of old Matt! You let me see to him instead, Peter. I'll rock him to sleep like a weakly lamb! It's only that violin that's scared

him. And that's a strange thing to be sure –
someone up here making such mournful music at
night!'

Matt walked into the dark caravan, making
soft, comforting noises in his deep, kind voice.
Peter flashed his torch swiftly inside, and saw
Benny's dark head on a pillow in a corner. Old
Matt bent over him.

The boys left the caravan in silence, and began
to walk home. They were filled with curiosity and
were extremely puzzled.

Peter spoke first. 'I don't understand all this. It
must have been Luke playing that violin somewhere on the hillside. But why? Matt seems quite
certain that he and Mrs Bolan went off to the
town, and left Benny in the van. They took the
baby with them, of course, as the pram is gone.
Well, then – why did Luke Bolan apparently come
back, all on his own, and play a violin?'

'I don't know,' said Colin. 'But I'm perfectly
certain in my own mind that it was Luke who
stole that violin, and uses it to comfort himself
with because his banjo has been burnt. He may
have left his wife down in the town for an hour or
two, and come up here to play it.'

'Well – where do you suppose he hides it?'
asked George. 'He must hide it very carefully

somewhere – because if it were found he'd go to prison for theft!'

'He probably hides it in his caravan, under the mattress – or in the bread-bin, or some such place,' said Peter. 'I think we ought to come up tomorrow and see if we can find it. Luke will be off to some fair or other, earning his living, and we know Mrs Bolan takes the baby and Benny to go shopping. Janet and I met her in the town the other morning.'

'All right. We'll come up here tomorrow,' said George. 'I feel as if I MUST get to the bottom of this. It's all so strange – the fire – the missing scarecrow clothes – the stolen violin – the wailing in the night – and yet no one about to play the violin!'

'Look out!' hissed Colin suddenly, and the three stopped walking very suddenly. A figure stood not far off, still and silent in the big field. Peter chuckled.

'Idiot! It's our old friend the scarecrow! I'm glad to see he's still wearing his new clothes. Come on – we shall all get into awful rows if we're much later!'

'What time shall we meet tomorrow?' asked George. 'Shall we all go – the whole Secret Seven? We'll take something up to the Bolans as an excuse for calling.'

'Right. As near ten o'clock as you can manage,'

said Peter. 'Then we can get back in good time for lunch.'

They parted at Peter's front gate and went to their homes, thinking over the night's adventure – for it really had been an adventure! All except that silly business when Susie and Binkie tried to upset everything!

'I hope to goodness they don't get to hear that we're going up to the caravan tomorrow,' thought George as he went home. 'Jack really ought to be more careful. He deserves to be chucked out of the Secret Seven if he can't keep Susie and her giggling friend in order!'

Jack somehow managed to keep Susie in complete ignorance of what was happening, and arrived at Peter's in good time the next morning. Everyone was there. A very brief meeting was held, at which Peter explained to the girls and to Jack exactly what had happened the night before. They listened in astonishment and envy, especially poor old Jack, who had had to escort Susie and Binkie home!

'Gosh – to think it was someone playing a *violin*!' said Jack. 'I wish I'd heard it. Bother Susie! I bet it was Luke Bolan playing it! Well – what a bad lot he is – smashing a window to steal a really valuable old violin!'

'Come on,' said Peter, standing up. 'Yes, you too, Scamper. Mother's given us some butter and biscuits to take up to Mrs Bolan, so they will make a nice excuse for seeing her, if she happens to be there. If she isn't we shall have a chance to look inside the van to see if the violin is tucked away somewhere.'

Off they all went, Scamper running beside them, his tongue hanging out. Where were the Secret Seven off to now? Scamper didn't care if they were going to the moon, so long as he could go with them!

18 An unexpected find

The Seven arrived at Matt's hut and looked inside it. The shepherd was not there – in fact, they could see him a long way off, rounding up sheep on the opposite hill. He waved to them and they waved back. His dog was with him, working hard.

'Now to see if the Bolans' van is empty,' said Peter, and they went across to it, carrying the biscuits and the butter. Scamper trotted on in front, his long tail waving happily to and fro.

'Mrs Bolan! Are you there?' called Peter. There was no answer at all.

'The pram's not here,' said Janet, sorry that she wouldn't see the dear little baby.

'Is the door locked?' asked Peter anxiously. 'I hope to goodness it isn't.' He ran up the steps and knocked. 'Mrs Bolan! Are you in?'

There was no answer. He pushed gently at the door, and it yielded, opening a little.

'I'll just put the butter and biscuits on the shelf!' he called to the others, and went right inside. The caravan smelt musty and rather unpleasant, and was not very tidy. The big mattress still lay on the floor, as if Mrs Bolan had left in a hurry and hadn't troubled to tidy anything. Even the dirty breakfast cups and plates were still left on the shelf.

'Can we come in too?' called Janet.

'No. I'll just have a quick hunt round myself, and then one of you can come in, and check round to see that I haven't missed any hiding-place,' said Peter. 'We'd get in each other's way if we all came in, it's so small. It shouldn't be difficult to find a violin hidden here.'

The others stood outside, some on the caravan steps, some on the grass, peering in to see what Peter was doing. He searched very thoroughly indeed.

'Nothing under or in the mattress!' he called. 'Nothing in the cupboard. Wait, there's a shelf almost in the roof of the caravan – there's a long box there – that might be it!'

He took down the box and opened it – but it was quite empty except for a few mildewed papers that might even have belonged to Matt, when *he* had the caravan!

Peter searched everywhere. Then he came to the door, rather disappointed. 'No go!' he said. 'The violin is definitely not here. I suppose it might be hidden under a bush somewhere – but I don't think so, because that would ruin it – even if it had a case, which it hasn't. The case was left behind in the shop. Janet – you come up and search.'

Janet leapt up the steps, and the others watched her searching too. Peter told Colin and Jack to look *under* the caravan as well, for there were a few things there. But no – the violin was certainly not among them. It was very, very disappointing.

Then suddenly Janet gave a loud squeal, and made everyone jump. 'What is it?' they cried.

'Look what I've found hanging behind the caravan door!' she cried. 'It was opened flat against the wall, and I didn't think of looking behind it till this moment. LOOK!'

And she displayed something very, very surprising to the rest of the Seven. Not the stolen violin – but the stolen scarecrow clothes!

Yes, there they were – the old tweed coat, the dirty hat, and grey flannel trousers!

Everyone stared in amazement, recognising the clothes at once.

'But – but – how did they come to be in the caravan?' said Janet.

'Easy! Luke stole them from the scarecrow, wore them as a disguise to steal the violin, then came back to the van and hung them behind the door!' said Jack. 'Who would bother about old clothes in a van? No one would know they once belonged to a scarecrow!'

'Oh dear!' said Pam. 'I can't help feeling awfully sorry for poor Mrs Bolan. I'm sure she didn't know Luke stole the scarecrow clothes – or the violin. Where *can* that violin be? It simply *must* be hidden somewhere!'

'Well, it's certainly not here,' said Peter. 'And as I'm sure it's not hidden in the bushes, there's only one place I can think of!'

'Where's that?' asked the others, eagerly.

'In the baby's pram,' said Peter. 'No one would ever think anything was hidden in such a place, certainly not a valuable violin. I bet that's where it's kept.'

'But Peter – it would ruin a violin to be bounced about on all day – and the baby is a very bouncy one!' said Pam.

'It could easily be wrapped round and round in some thick material,' said Peter. 'Easily! I bet I'm right!'

'Well – what do we do *now*, then?' asked Colin. 'We *think* Luke stole the scarecrow clothes to disguise himself – we *think* he stole that violin because his banjo was burnt – we *think* he plays it out on the hills at night – and now we *think* it's hidden in the baby's pram. But we can't prove a single thing!'

'If we could only look inside the pram, we should know,' said Jack.

'But how can we do that?' asked Peter.

'Sh!' said Jack suddenly. 'Look who's coming!'

They turned in a hurry – and saw Mrs Bolan hurrying along with the baby in the pram. It was howling loudly. Benny ran by his mother's side, holding on to the pram.

At first Mrs Bolan didn't see the children beside the caravan. Peter shut the door hurriedly, and then they all went towards her, hardly knowing what to say.

'There, there, little love,' she was saying to the baby. 'You're starving, aren't you, poor lamb!' She picked it up and turned to take it to the caravan, suddenly startled to see the seven children. She tried to smile her usual smile – but her face was worried and anxious, quite without its usual cheerful expression.

'Why, good morning, my dears,' she said. 'I'm just going to feed the baby. I've been down the town all the morning, and she's starving, poor mite. I meant to be back before this!'

She hurried into the caravan, and Benny went too.

'What about looking into the pram now?' said Pam, in a low voice. 'It's our only chance. Oh – I DO hope the violin isn't there!'

She bent over the pram and pulled away a dirty covering. Peter burrowed deep down into the wall of the pram, surprised to find his fingers trembling. He felt something long and hard, wrapped in thick cloth! He pulled it out.

He unwrapped a little of the cloth – and part of a violin handle showed at once! 'Yes – it *is* the violin!' said Peter, shocked. 'Now what do we do?'

19   Little Benny

A loud voice made all the Secret Seven jump. They looked up, to see a man walking up to them – a tall, stooping fellow, with thick black hair and eyes exactly like Benny's – Luke Bolan. He looked very angry.

'You give me that! Poking and prying! I'll box your ears, the lot of you!'

'Are you Luke Bolan?' said Peter. 'Well, isn't this the violin that was stolen from the antique shop?'

There was a scream from behind them, and Mrs Bolan came flying out of the caravan. Benny behind her.

'Luke! Luke! Leave those children be! Don't you dare harm them. Oh, look at that now – they've found the violin!' And to the children's utter dismay, she covered her face with her hands and began to sob. Benny began to sob, too, in fright, pulling at her dress.

Luke took the violin roughly from Peter, and held it up in the air as if he were going to dash it to the ground and break it. But Mrs Bolan held his arm at once.

'No, Luke, no. That would only make things worse. What do you children know about this? How did you find out?'

'It's too long a tale to tell,' said Peter. 'But Colin here actually saw your husband smash the window and take the violin – and he saw that he was wearing our old scarecrow's clothes: and I'm afraid we've just seen them hanging in your caravan. And now, of course, we've found the violin!'

'Oh Luke, Luke, what have you done to us?' wept Mrs Bolan. 'You'll go to prison, sure as the sun is in the sky – and then what's to happen to me and the children? All our things burnt – and me left with the baby and poor little Benny!'

Luke put his arms round her, looking very sad indeed. Mrs Bolan flashed round on the children.

'I was going to put back that violin in the shop this very morning! Yes, that I was – and Luke here, he'll tell you the same. We didn't know it was so valuable! Luke thought it was so old-looking that it wasn't worth much!'

'I see,' said Peter, suddenly understanding. 'Of course – it does look very, very old. But didn't Luke see the notice beside it?'

'Yes,' said Luke. 'But that didn't mean anything to me.'

'Luke can't read,' said Mrs Bolan, wiping her eyes. 'He never went to school – he lived in a caravan all the time he was a child, and wasn't anywhere long enough to get schooling. If he'd have seen the notice and read how old and precious the violin was, he'd never have taken it – would you, Luke?'

'No, I wouldn't,' said Luke. 'I never thought it was worth more than a few pounds – and I'd not got even those, after our shack caught fire. I meant to go in and pay later. But I needed that violin so badly.'

'Why? Just because your banjo was burnt?' asked Colin, rather scornfully.

'Banjo? No, I didn't care so much about *that*!' said Luke, surprised. 'I can always borrow a banjo. No, young man, it was for my Benny I wanted the violin.'

'Benny! But – surely he can't play a violin!' cried Janet, amazed.

'Benny, love – do you want to give us a tune?' said Mrs Bolan, bending over the scared-looking little boy. He couldn't understand what was going on, and he was very frightened. Why was his mother crying?

Luke took the violin from the pram, where he had laid it when he went to comfort his wife. He put it into the eager little hands that went out for it – Benny's small brown hands, that seemed to come alive when they felt the smoothness of the old violin.

He walked a little way away, and stood with his back to them. He put the violin under his chin, and raised the bow – and on the air came once again that strange 'wailing', unearthly and beautiful, that the boys had heard the night before. No tune – just a series of beautiful sounds as if Benny was singing his own strange thoughts.

'He's playing to himself – just as the blackbird sings to himself, listening all the time,' thought Janet.

'No, no, Benny – play "The Dancing May-Tree!"' called his mother. 'Not your own tunes!'

And straightaway the boy swept into the merriest, lightest dance that the children had ever heard – joyous, breath-taking, astonishing. They gasped in wonder.

Mrs Bolan smiled round at them. 'There! That's an old gipsy tune. Benny plays them all! My little Benny! You've never heard him play, have you? He . . .'

'Well – we did hear him last night, when it was

dark,' said Peter. 'And old Matt heard him the night before. But he only played that kind of *wailing* music of his own, and Matt was puzzled and told us about it.'

'So we came up last night to see if we could hear it too – and we did,' said Colin. 'But we knew at once that it was someone playing a violin most beautifully. And we guessed the violin was a very good one – the stolen one, in fact!'

'Oh Benny, Benny – and I left you asleep in bed!' said Mrs Bolan. 'And so I did the night before. You got out of bed, found the violin and took it out to play on the hillside – is that what you did?'

Benny didn't answer. He didn't even turn to face his mother. He was rubbing the bow gently on the strings, making a curious sound like the wind in the trees. Janet suddenly realised that that was exactly what he *was* playing – the actual little song that the wind was whispering in the nearby birch-tree!

'But he's a genius!' she thought. 'I hardly know which is the violin and which is the wind.' Then she spoke out loud.

'Mrs Bolan! Benny's wonderful! He's a little genius! Oh, why don't you send him to school? Why don't you let him be taught music properly?'

'Benny wouldn't be any good at school, Miss,' said Mrs Bolan, and she drew the child to her. 'Why, surely you know what's the matter with him? My Benny is blind.'

Blind! Now the children knew why those great dark eyes had no expression in them, and why Benny was so careful when he walked! Poor, poor little Benny.

'Music is the only thing that keeps him happy,' said Mrs Bolan. 'And when he lost his own violin in the fire it seemed as if his heart was broken. That's why Luke took that old violin – just to make our little Benny happy again!'

20 Meeting of the Secret Nine!

The Seven looked at Mrs Bolan, and then at the silent mysterious little Benny. Janet felt tears coming to her eyes. What could they do to help this gifted little boy? SOMEthing must be done! But the Secret Seven couldn't do it. No, the grown-ups must come into this – they always knew what to do!

And so it was that the Seven went to Peter's father and mother that morning, and poured out the whole story to them.

'We don't know what to do now, Mother,' said Peter, when the tale was ended. 'The violin must go back to the shop – but Daddy, poor Luke mustn't be put into prison! Benny must go to school, and he *must* be taught music – and he must have a violin of his own. The Secret Seven are quite prepared to buy one for him, even if they have to save for a year.'

'You're a good set of kids,' said his father, pleased. 'This is a most remarkable story, I must say! I don't know how you Seven get mixed up in things of this sort! Now first, about the violin. We can quite well give it back without any harm coming to Luke. Matt tells me he's a good enough fellow – and I don't expect he would have stolen that violin if he hadn't been so upset at Benny's being burnt.'

'He simply loves Benny!' said Pam. 'But how can the violin be given back without Luke coming into it?'

'There's a reward offered for its return – and if returned in good condition, no questions will be asked,' said Peter's father. 'I proposed to take it back myself, and say that I can't explain how it came into my possession – but that the man who took it is very sorry – and naturally I could not take any reward. That should settle that.'

'Oh good!' said all the Secret Seven, and then Scamper thumped his tail on the floor.

'And what about Benny?' asked Janet.

'I think I can help there,' said her mother. 'He can go to one of the schools run for blind children, and his gift for music will be developed to the utmost. He won't mind so much leaving his mother if he can have his precious music, and he will have all his holidays with her, of course!'

'Oh, thank goodness!' said Barbara and Pam, together. It had been a terrible shock to the Seven to learn that little Benny, with his beautiful dark eyes, was blind. But now it wouldn't matter so much – he would always be happy with his music!

'Well – it isn't often the Secret Seven have a Secret *Nine* meeting!' said Peter's father, smiling. 'I must say that Mummy and I feel highly honoured, Peter. Grown-ups are quite a help sometimes, aren't they?'

'Oh Daddy – we couldn't do without you!' cried Janet, and gave him a sudden hug. 'Do you *mind* taking the violin back to the shop? You're sure you won't be arrested?'

'Quite sure,' said her father. 'And what's more, if the Secret Seven really do mean to get money together to buy little Benny a violin, I'd like to help too – and so would Mummy, of course. I could have a look at the violins in the music shop, and see if there's one that would suit a small boy – so that Benny won't fret for his own burnt one any more.'

'Oh YES!' cried all the Seven together, and Scamper thumped his tail once more. He had no idea what was going on, but he was certainly enjoying it all. What other dog in the world would be allowed in at an important secret meeting like this?

Peter's father lost no time in dealing with the violin. He never told the Seven exactly what had passed between him and the antique-shop dealer – he merely said that all was well, and that Luke's name had not been mentioned.

'But I shall have a word or two with Luke myself,' he said. 'Just to make sure that he knows he was *almost* in very serious trouble.'

'Have you got another violin for Benny?' asked Janet anxiously.

'You can go up to Mrs Bolan and tell her to take Benny down to the music shop tomorrow, and they will let him try their smaller ones,' said Daddy. 'And then bring her here for Mummy to talk to her about school for Benny. Dear me, we do seem to be meddling in other people's affairs!'

'Not meddling – just giving a helping hand!' said his wife. 'As for the Secret Seven, Peter, you'll have to keep them all up to the mark, you know – and help to pay for Benny's violin!'

The Seven kept their word, of course. They had never in their lives been so busy earning money in holiday time! They found themselves jobs of all kinds, and even Susie joined in!

'Binkie's gone home, thank goodness,' said Jack. 'So Susie is just a bit more sensible. Mother says we're to allow her to get a job and give us the money if she wants to. She says it will do Susie good.'

'Oh well – if it's possible to do Susie good by all means let her work hard!' said Peter. 'But all the same, she is NOT going to come to our next Secret Seven meeting.'

When the day of the meeting came, two days before they went back to school, what a pile of money they had to count – plenty to buy the violin that Benny was already very, very happy with! He was to take it to the blind school with him, and that pleased him very much.

'Well – you've all worked very hard,' said Peter, looking round at the Seven. 'It's been rather exciting, hasn't it? Thanks for all your money, Secret Seven. Oh, and here's a bit more.' He emptied several coins on to the upturned box in front of him.

'Who's that from? Susie?' asked George.

'No. It's from Scamper!' answered Peter, with a laugh. 'He gave up two large bones and one little one in order to help Benny – and here's his money! Thanks most awfully, Scamper! You're a brick!'

'Wuff!' said Scamper happily. 'Wuff-wuff-wuff-wuff-wuff!'

'He says it's a pleasure to help us!' said Peter solemnly. 'And he really *does* like the Secret Seven!'

So do we, Peter. So do we!

THE ENID BLYTON NEWSLETTER

Would you like to receive The Enid Blyton Newsletter? It has lots of news about Enid Blyton books, videos, plays, etc. There are also puzzles and a page for your letters. It is published three times a year and is free for children who live in the United Kingdom and Ireland.

If you would like to receive it for a year, please write to: The Enid Blyton Newsletter, PO Box 357, London WC2E 9HQ, sending your name and address. (UK and Ireland only)